This book is dedicated to SBR Publications, TeamBankrollSquad and every person who has supported me thus far... and those that will.

Love... KING

Acknowledgments

I literally sat for hours contemplating on what to write for this author's note/acknowledgments. Finally I said to myself, Fu** it, write what's in your heart. So here we go. First and foremost, God is to be thanked for all things being. Secondly, my loving mother, Marion Johnson; without you there is no us. A true UNION starts in the heart. To my two sisters, Keisha & Latrice and my four brothers, Boss, Jah, Matic & Marv. I love all of you, unconditionally! One day we'll all be able to sit at the same table to eat and share memories together. To my immediate family, aunts, cousins, uncles, nieces & nephews, you all support me and that love is very much appreciated. To Lovey... For being the strong, caring individual you are. I love you and always will. I want to send a special shout out to my cousin, Ralph aka K.O. in Clinton Correctional.

Hold your head fam. We love you and we're here for you every step of the way. the readers of my past work and new readers who are picking up a book with my name on it for the first time. There are no words to express the gratitude I feel when someone tells me they read and liked my work. I truly appreciate the support I get from my readers. Y'all are the BEST! You guys are my motivation to keep pushing my thoughts to the limit. As long as you continue to read, I'll continue writing. It's love and this love comes straight from the heart. To my hood, Hartley Housing! I went from playing tag in the front of the buildings, to hustling drugs inside the buildings. I knew it was wrong, but I had a purpose. Maybe every intention wasn't positive, but along the way I was able to receive mass amounts of knowledge and structure from being in those streets and choosing that life. I did my dirt, paid my dues and respectively bowed out. I'll never be the one to judge another person on what they do or the way they do it. All I can offer is the knowledge I was given. There is a different way, but it's up to YOU to make the decision. Be smart! And of course I can't forget **TEAMBANKROLLSQUAD!** It's not a gang. It's a lifestyle!! We are the strongest team in AA fiction. Yeah, I said it! We stick together as a family and great things happen. Together we are an UNSTOPPABLE FORCE! I love y'all! David Weaver, thank you for giving me the opportunity and the platform to showcase my work. I am truly humbled and honored to be a part of this **TBRS** family. It's loyalty & love bro...till the END! Tina Nance, you're a wonderful editor and a beautiful person inside and out. Thank you! I knew we'd be working together sooner than later! #1 let's get it!!

"You either stay by my side and walk step for step with me to the top or fall behind and get left in the dust. Regardless of your intentions; I will make my mark." ~KING

Also available by Tremayne Johnson

A Drug Dealer's Dream

King

DAVID WEAVER PRESENTS
THE UNION
LET NO ONE STAND BEFORE WE
A NOVEL BY
TREMAYNE JOHNSON

Hit me up on Facebook or follow me on Twitter!

www.facebook.com/tremaynej

www.twitter.com/GS914

ONE

June, 1995

The tattered, decrepit building on 1st and 3rd street in Mt. Vernon, New York was a dugout for the hustlers and a smoke haven for the addicts. Hundreds of empty crack vials lay scattered along the urine filled steps. Graffiti ridden staircase walls held the names of those past and present and the stench of marijuana lingered through the air, but still, this was home, a sanctuary to more than fifty families.

Three flights up, in an undersized, cluttered apartment, the soothing melody of Mary J Blige's *"My Life"* and the scent of hamburgers and French fries escaped into the hallway.

Sybil snatched open the refrigerator door in search of the last bit of ketchup, but the bottle was empty.

"Cleo!" She yelled.

"Yes??"

"Go over to your aunt's and get some ketchup."

His shoulders sulked and his once playful expression turned grim. "Aww, ma... I don't wanna go over there." he pouted.

Sybil walked into the living room and stood in front of the television. "I ain't asking you, I'm telling you, now get your ass up and go next door."

Cleo shook his head and poked his lips out. He hated going across the hall to his aunt Wanda's house, it was overrun with roaches.

"But they got roaches, Ma."

Sybil didn't like when Cleo said things like that. Even though she was slightly better off financially than her little sister, she never acted as if she was superior. They were both stuck in the hood.

"So do we; this apartment ain't no better than theirs. I told you about talking like that."

Cleo's reason for not wanting to go next door wasn't really the roaches, it was his cousin Mox. The truth is; his fear was being fueled by his own insecurity. He was very aware that Mox is smarter, faster, and stronger than he is, but

Mox was naïve, hesitant, and unconscious of his own abilities.

He put his sneakers on and went to do what his mother asked.

"Who is it!?" Wanda screamed from the bathroom when she heard someone knocking at the front door.

"I got it Ma!"

Mox put the controller down, got up from the futon, checked the peephole and then swung the door open, letting his cousin Cleo in.

"Cleo, wassup?"

"Wassup." He mumbled, and then nodded at Casey.

The pungent order of sensimilla invaded Cleo's nostrils instantly, and then a cockroach the size of a small Bic lighter darted across the 20 inch television set grabbing his attention, but Mox paid it no mind.

"You scared of a little roach Cleo?" he joked seeing the fear in his eyes.

"Nah, I'm sayin'... that joint was big."

"Whatever... Yo! Them joints is hot!" he shouted, looking down at Cleo's new, white, grey and red Air Max. "Let me rock your old joints since you got those?"

"Nah..."

"C'mon Cleo..." he begged. " You said you was gon' look out for me."

"I did look out for you. I gave you those black sneakers."

Mox reached underneath the grubby futon and pulled out a pair of black, soiled Reeboks.

"I been wearing these every day for more than a year." He said, shaking his head.

Cleo wasn't concerned with how long Mox had been wearing the sneakers; he was still upset at the fact that his mother made him give up a pair of his old ones. If he had it his way, Mox would be walking on his bare feet.

Any opportunity Cleo had to be better than Mox, he took full advantage of. He knew morally it was incorrect, but he wasn't able to shake his envious characteristics. It came from his heart, so it was in his blood.

Switching the subject, Cleo asked, "Y'all got some ketchup?"

Mox went into the kitchen, grabbed the ketchup and squeezed some into a plastic cup.

He held up the cup. "Is this enough?"

The cockroach that was once on the television skirted across Cleo's sneaker, he panicked and his arm brushed against the vase sitting on the mantle, knocking it to the floor.

"Ooooh..." Casey crooned.

Mox raised his index finger to his lips. "Shhh... be quiet, Casey."

The crash rattled Wanda's nerves. She reached to pull her pants up and almost knocked the small mirror off the sink. The bathroom door was locked and she was puffing a joint and sniffing a line of coke.

"Mox, what the fuck was that!?" She hollered.

"Damn, Cleo... you just broke her favorite vase." He looked down at the shattered pieces on the floor. "Go head man, take the ketchup and go before she comes out here."

"What you gon' tell her?" He said, opening the front door.

"It don't matter... I'ma still get my ass whooped."

The bathroom door flew open and the front door closed.

Cleo was gone.

"What was that noise?" Wanda asked.

She looked to her youngest, and then down at Mox picking up shattered pieces of her favorite vase.

"I know that ain't my vase, Mox!?"

He was too afraid to make eye contact. "I knocked it over by accident, ma." He lied, and that was something he never did.

Wanda's lip curled as it did every time she became angry. She screwed her eyes, balled her fist and shot a sharp, right hook to his ribs. "Get the fuck up and get yo' ass in that room... and take them goddamn pants off!"

Mox absorbed the blow and did as told.

At ten years old, he was accustomed to the beatings, so eventually, he learned to block out the pain and visualize more pleasant occasions; but those fantasies never lasted long.

He closed the bedroom door, stripped to his bare skin and waited to endure another lashing. He was cool about it though, his only concern was what her weapon of choice would be today.

The iron?

A wire hanger?

Or maybe that bamboo broom Aunt Sybil brought back from Japan?

Either way, he didn't mind taking the ass whooping for his cousin, he thought nothing of it, he felt it was his duty to take the blame because he knew Cleo was scared. His little brother Casey didn't like seeing him get in trouble, he loved his big brother, so he sat back on the dingy futon, crying till he could make no more tears. He rocked himself to sleep.

LATER THAT NIGHT

Wailing screams at 2:30 am woke Mox and Casey from their sleep.

"What was that?" Casey jumped up, wiping the crust from his eyes.

"I don't know. Wait here, I'll be right back."

He begged "No, Mox... don't leave me." Jumping out the bed, he followed his big brother.

The room was pitch black as Mox and Casey silently tip toed to the bedroom door. Mox turned the doorknob slowly and took a peek into the hallway. It was too dark to see, but he could hear someone's voice, they were saying a prayer.

"If we confess our sins, he is faithful and just—" As they got closer to the living room, the rumbling vocal sound grew louder, "—And will forgive us our sins and purify us from all unrighteousness..."

The sour scent of blood perfumed the air and irritated Mox's nose. His stomach muscles tightened and a sudden sweat fell over his body. He fought the urge to vomit and before reaching the entrance to the living room, he stopped short and Casey was on his heels.

“Casey, wait right here,” he whispered. “Don’t move.”

Mox crept through the static dimness; his midnight skin tone merging perfectly with the blackness. Now only a few steps from the living room, he sensed something wrong and wanted to turn back, but his feet continued to move forward. When he entered the living room, the sight before his eyes churned his insides and the vomit he suppressed only seconds ago erupted through his lips.

His father’s butchered, unclothed body was draped over the futon, his hands were tied behind his back in a pipe hitch knot which is used primarily by boy scouts and his throat was slit.

Mox was unable to move. Paralyzed, he watched the tall, wide body, dark skinned assassin hover over his mother’s defenseless, naked figure. The twelve inch blade he gripped securely, was called a Tanto and it was soaked in blood.

Wanda lay stretched across the floor in the middle of the small, filthy apartment, choking on her own blood. She had suffered thirty five stab wounds to the face, chest and neck.

Casey startled his big brother when he brushed up against his arm and attempted to glance over his shoulder.

Mox went to shield his eyes from the horrendous scene, but Casey was determined to see.

They stood, bare chested and barefoot in their underwear, innocent; focused on the woman who pushed them from her womb, as she gagged, taking her last breaths before their sinless eyes.

The killer slowly turned to the young boys. “Mox,” he muttered, wiping the bloody sword onto his sleeve.

“Everything comes to an end.” He looked at Wanda, bent down, put his hand over her face and closed her eyes. “Sleep baby...” he whispered, then made his exit.

2002

A milky, drop, CLK 430 crept along the jagged, pothole filled pavement slowing down at the corner of Horton Avenue and Brook Street. The lambent rays from the early morning sun made the polished white paint look like glass.

Wise Earl and two young wolves were holding the block down on this early morning. They watched the glossy, two door convertible pull to the curb and park.

"You young niggas don't know shit about gettin' this money." Earl hissed. The temperature was almost at a hundred degrees and the air was sticky, condensed and humid.

He wiped the sweat from his brow and took a long drag of his cigarette. "Now this nigga here," he said, pointing to the car, "that nigga gettin' that real paper."

The passenger side door opened and one of the sexiest creatures God ever created stepped out. Her olive complexion was radiant and her skin was flawless. The tight fitted, pink shorts she was wearing cupped her dainty, heart shaped ass cheeks perfectly and her well-formed c-cup breast bounced with each step.

Priscilla was a Goddess. She had recently cut her hair short and was rocking the natural look. It completely fit her personality.

She pranced around the front of the vehicle with a bag in her hand. Her cupid shaped, berry colored lips looked juicy enough to bite.

The young wolves gawked at her glowing beauty.

Wise Earl shook his head at their actions. “See... that’s the problem wit’ you young niggas, you worried ‘bout some pussy when you need to focus on the come up.”

The beautiful young lady approached Earl.

“Wassup, Uncle Wise?”

“Hey, baby girl.” He answered, embracing her. She smelled wonderful. “Tell that nigga to roll the window down.”

Earl tossed his hands up and the driver side window slowly came down.

"Uncle Wise, what's good?"

"You tell me, nephew. I know you better step out that goddamn car and come give your uncle some love."

Mox pushed the door open and got out.

He was no longer the short, skinny dark skinned kid he was seven years ago. He was grown up now, 6 feet 2 inches, black as the dead of night and in control of his own operation.

He hugged his uncle and dapped the young wolves.

"What's the word, Unc?"

Earl plucked the remnants of his cigarette and looked at Mox. "The only thing more threatenin' to you besides your enemy, is the people closest to you. Never forget that."

Mox nodded and walked into the corner store. He came out with a bottled water and the newspaper.

"Priscilla," He said, getting back in the car. "Get that and let's go."

She unzipped the small Gucci carrying bag and handed it to Earl.

“Go fill that up, youngin’.”

One of the young wolves took the bag and went around the corner. He returned in seconds handing the bag back to Priscilla.

“You been upstairs, Unc?” Mox asked, ready to pull off.

“Earlier, she up there wit’ Casey and Cleo. I’ll be through in a minute.”

“Aight.”

Mox pulled from the curb and made the right down Brook Street and then he made another right into the lot and pulled in a parking space.

They got out the car, walked to building 80 and took the elevator to the sixth floor.

He stood in front of 6A fumbling through his pocket for the keys, finally finding them and opening the door.

As soon as it opened Casey jumped into Mox’s arms.

“Whoa, boy; you getting too big to be doing that. Wassup?”

"Nothing." Casey, jumped back down to the floor. He picked his basketball up and continued dribbling.

"Casey!" Cleo yelled from the back room. "Stop bouncing that ball in the house!"

"Shut up!" Mox yelled back.

"Who dat!?"

"Who you want it to be!?"

"What I tell y'all 'bout all that damn noise in my house." Sybil added. She was in the kitchen washing dishes.

Cleo came from the back room.

"It's this little nigga." He snarled, snatching the basketball from Casey.

"Hey!"

"Hey, nothin'... I told you 'bout this ball. I don't know why you always got it anyway, you ain't no good."

Mox took the ball from Cleo and gave it back to Casey. "Leave my lil' brother alone. Tell him, Casey... you going to the NBA."

Casey's eyes lit up and he got excited. "Yup! And when I get rich, I'ma buy Mox a house and Auntie a house and you ain't getting' nothing 'cause you always bothering me."

Cleo mushed the 12 year old making him stumble into the dining table and Casey threw the ball, striking him in his stomach, then he ran through the house.

"You lil' muthafucka!" He growled, ready to chase after him.

"Chill, Cleo." Mox grabbed his arm.

"Get the fuck off me." He yanked away, cursing. "Priscilla, why you hang around this nigga, I know you can do better than this asshole."

Sybil slammed a dish in the sink. "Cleo, watch your mouth in my house!"

"It's this nigga." He pouted.

"It's always somebody else, it's never you." She said, drying off the last dish. "How you doing, Priscilla?"

"Hello, Ms. Daniels. I'm good." She took a seat at the table.

"Why you always sticking up for him? You aint never on my side." Cleo whined.

"Cleo, cut the bullshit and get ready for practice."

He pouted his lips and turned to walk away. He knew better than to talk back.

"Wassup, Auntie?" Mox hugged his aunt. "How's everything?"

"I'm surviving, baby, blessed to see another day."

He glanced around the kitchen. It was always a homely feeling when he stepped through the door. He appreciated his aunt stepping up and taking care of him and his brother. If it wasn't for her, they would have been dragged into foster care and more than likely, they would have been split up.

After his parents were killed, Sybil took full custody of her sister's two boys. Since then, Mox had moved out on his own, but Casey was still here.

His eyes fell to a picture that was stuck on the refrigerator.

"Do you miss her, Auntie?" He stared at one of the few visual memories of his mother.

"Miss who, Mox?"

"My mother..."

Sybil turned and faced Mox. "Of course I miss her. I think about her every day."

"I do too... you know something," Mox opened the refrigerator and grabbed the pitcher of Kool-Aid. "I wanted to ask you this for the longest, but I was always afraid of the answer."

"Ask me what?"

Mox leaned against the wall. He needed some closure, seven years was long enough.

"Do you remember that night?"

She sighed. "Like it was yesterday."

"Do you know why it happened?"

"I don't have a clue, Mox. I wish I did." She peeled the picture off the refrigerator. "I really miss my sister." Her eyes got watery and a tear rolled down her cheek.

Mox ripped a paper towel from the roll that was on the counter and handed it to her.

"Lately it's been on my mind. It just bothers me that nobody knows anything."

Sybil listened to Mox. She knew more than she led him to believe, but she was afraid to expose her dark secrets.

"Sometimes the truth can cause pain, baby."

"No more than it's already caused—."

A knock at the door disturbed their conversation.

"Who is it?"

"Open up lil' nigga."

Mox unlocked the door and Wise Earl strolled into the apartment.

He looked around the peaceful room. Something was going on. It was too quiet for this to be his sister's house.

"What the hell is going on in here? Why y'all lookin' so sad?"

"Uncle Wise, I was just asking auntie if she knew anything about the night my mother and father got killed."

Earl was shocked. His eyes moved from Sybil to Mox, and then back to Sybil. He didn't expect to walk in on a subject so personal. He could tell his older sister had been crying.

"Mox, sometimes things happen and we can't do anything about it. That's life."

"Naw, Unc... I ain't tryna hear that."

"Well, that's what it is."

"That ain't what it is, Uncle Wise. Listen to what you saying, basically you gave up. Y'all don't even care about what happened."

"It's not that I don't care, because I do. That was my sister, I love her, but—"

Mox cut in. "But what, Unc?"

The room went silent.
"I believe if y'all did know something y'all would tell me..." There was a pause. "Right?" he glanced back and forth. "C'mon, Priscilla." Mox hugged his aunt. "I'm old enough to

know now Auntie, and if somebody doesn't tell me, eventually I'll find out on my own," he said.

Earl grabbed his nephew's arm and brought him in close. "I love you boy. Be safe out there, Mox."

"I got you, Unc. Hey, Auntie, tell Casey I'll be through at nine o'clock tomorrow so I can take him to his game."

He walked out the door and Priscilla followed.

Wise Earl shook his head and then looked at his sister. "You gon' have to tell him one day, sis."

TWO

Priscilla and Mox's unity began only two years prior. It was the summer of 2000 and the upcoming school year, young Mox would become a freshman at New Rochelle high school. At the time he was into sports heavy, baseball and track and field were the ones he favored.

Currently under his Aunt Sybil's care, it was a struggle for her to raise three growing boys. Things were tight, but they managed to get through.

All three of the boys played sports, so the refrigerator was always empty and the laundry was always dirty.

Mox took it upon himself to go out and find a part time job washing cars down at the Shiny Gleam car wash in Mamaroneck, which was about ten minutes away. Most the staff was illegal immigrants and young black kids Mox's age, so they didn't mind working with him as long as he did what he was asked.

He made a few dollars every week and was able to contribute to the household, contrary to how to his cousin Cleo saw things. He figured he didn't need to work because in a few years he was going pro. But that was in a few years, this was now and Mox was not only pulling the weight of he and his brother, but also Cleo. He never once complained.

It was the top of the morning on a 96 degree summer day when the dark blue Honda Coupe with five star rims and an awful paint job turned into the car wash.

Mox arrived to work fifteen minutes earlier after having an argument with Cleo over the bathroom. Rather than a fist fight, he walked away, figuring he'd be the sensible one.

The blue Honda was the first car to pull up. It was only 8:50 and they usually didn't start washing cars till 9:15, but when the passenger side window came down Mox approached the pretty creature sitting behind it.

He smiled bright and asked, "Welcome to Shiny Gleam. How can I help you today?"

She smiled back, but the driver answered. "Fuck is you smiling for nigga? Lemme get the full wash, Armor All and all that... how much?"

"Would you like the interior done, sir?"

"Aint that part of the full wash? I said full wash!"

Mox stayed cool. "No it isn't sir, that's why I'm asking."

The driver became annoyed. "I don't want no extra shit, jus gimme the full wash... and make sure you put Armor All on my shit! Last time them fuckin' Mexicans got me."

Mox continued to ignore his obnoxiousness. He wrote out the receipt and passed it to the pretty female.

"Pull up to the yellow line and I'll take it from there."

Once the driver put the car in park, he hopped out and went inside to pay for the wash. His beautiful accomplice stood outside.

Mox used this opportunity to strike a conversation.

"Is that your boyfriend?" He inquired.

She didn't even look in his direction. "No."

"Then why you riding with him?"

"Little boy, you need to mind your business. Don't worry about why I'm riding with him."

Mox admired her from head to toe. She was perfect. Her mesmerizing eyes spoke volumes and he was feeling her sense of style. He knew she was older because of the way she dressed. She wore zebra print leggings that showed off her firm thighs, shiny red pumps that accentuated her calf muscles and a tight fitting, short sleeve shirt that emphasized her well-formed breasts.

“What’s your name beautiful?”

She smirked. “Why you wanna know my name?”

“I’m sayin’... I’m just being formal.” He extended his hand. “Mox Daniels.” He said.

“Priscilla Davis.” She replied, shaking his hand. “Aint you Cleo’s cousin?”

“Yeah... Priscilla,” He paused. “I like that name, it fits you.”

“Thank you.”

“You’re welcome. How old are you Priscilla?”

“Older than you.” She remarked.

“That won’t be a problem. I like older women.”

They laughed.

"I love your enthusiasm." She said, getting ready to get back into the car. The detailer was wiping the last tire down with Armor All. "Keep it up, you'll find what you're looking for."

"I already did." He responded.

Out the corner of his eye Mox saw the driver coming out to his car. He recognized the light skinned skinny kid, but he couldn't figure out his name. He was a halftime hustler from the other side of town.

"Yo!" the driver shouted. He had watched Priscilla and Mox talk the entire time. "Why the fuck is you even talkin' to this lame ass nigga?"

"Dee, shut up and get in the car." Priscilla replied.

Dee. That was his name. Deandre Foster.

Mox knew exactly who he was now. Deandre's younger brother is the same age as Mox and Dee is only two years older than both of them.

Once again, he ignored the slick talk and continued to do his work. He would see Priscilla another day and when he did, he would be determined to get her. As for Dee, he wasn't a bit worried about him. Mox already knew who the victor would be if it came down to a one on one.

As they pulled away from the car wash, Priscilla gave Mox a tasteful look and winked her eye. At that point, he knew he had her.

A few days later, a black Lexus GS 300 with stock rims and dark tint slowly pulled into the car wash.

Mox got up from the crate he was sitting on and hurried to the car.

The driver let the window down halfway.

"Welcome to Shiny Gleam. How can I help you today?" Mox smiled.

The window came all the way down and his smile grew bigger. "What's up beautiful?"

"Can you take off for lunch?" She asked.

Mox turned to see where his supervisor was. "Hold on." He shouted to his co-worker. "Yo, Javier! I'm taking an early lunch, you want a sandwich!?"

"Aight! Yeah, bring me one back!"

Mox tossed the drying towel he was holding into the bin and went around to the passenger side of the luxury vehicle.

"This joint is nice." He ran his fingers along the custom wood-grain paneling and inhaled the fresh scent of the new leather.

"Thank you," She shifted the gear to reverse and backed out of Shiny Gleam.

"Is this your man's car?" Mox watched as she maneuvered the sedan. Her finger nails were manicured and polished light pink and her hair was in its natural curly state.

"No, this is not my man's car. I told you, I don't have a man and for the record, this is my car."

"This car cost sixty-thousand dollars and you telling me it's yours."

"How do you know the price of this car?"

"I specialize in cars and women." He laughed.

"Is that right?" She was already in love with his humor. "Sixty-thousand dollars ain't a lot of money." She boasted.

"To who?"

"What if I told you that you could make sixty-thousand dollars in one night?"

Mox looked at her in disbelief. "What I gotta do?" He was anxious.

Priscilla chuckled. "Just like that, huh? No questions asked."

"Maybe, one."

"And what would that be?"

"Would I have to kill anybody for it?"

For a moment, Priscilla didn't say a word; she just focused on the road in front of her. Twenty feet ahead, she came to a stop at a red light.

She answered. "Only if you want to."

That day Priscilla and Mox ate lunch together at Subway and then she dropped him back off at work.

Even though she was three years older than he was, Priscilla really liked Mox and the feeling was something new to her. She was rarely interested in guys her age, let alone someone younger than she was, but Mox was different. It was something about his ambience that caught her attention the first time they met. He was truly eager and confident, not to mention his cockiness was attractive.

After a few dinner dates and two trips to the movies, Priscilla invited Mox over to her apartment.

The grey cab pulled up to the huge building on Pelham Road.

"760." The driver said. "That'll be six and a quarter."

Mox paid the fare and stepped out into the summery night air. He was rocking a dark blue pair of Guess jean shorts, a white short sleeve, three-button polo shirt and his brand new white on white Air Force Ones.

He walked into the building and looked for Priscilla's last name on the intercom list. She told him the buzzer number, but it slipped his mind that fast.

Searching through the long list of tenants, he finally spotted her name.

Davis. He said to himself. He lined his finger up with the name and slid it across to find out the apartment number.

Seeing it was *7C,* he pushed it and waited.

"Who is it?"

"Mox."

The buzzer sounded and he was able to enter the well-lit lobby. The view he took in was surprising, he marveled at how nice the building was. He had become used to the debris filled hallways and urine drenched elevators of the projects, but this was a world away from that and it was only five minutes away from the hood.

Mox checked his outfit in the large, rectangular wall mirror and then rode the elevator to the seventh floor. He followed the sign on the wall and made the right toward *7A-7E*.

When he got to the door, he could hear music, it was cracked open for him to walk right in.

Damn this is nice. The luscious scent of herbs and spices tickled his nose, admiring the paintings on the wall; he noticed each one of them was of African American people.

Mox took a few more steps down the hallway and into the living room where Donell Jones' *Where I Wanna Be* boomed through the surround sound.

"This is that joint!" Mox sang along.

Girl, the love that we share is real

But in time your heart will heal

I'm not saying I'm gone but I

Have to find what life is like

Without you...

Priscilla heard Mox's voice and was moved. She joined in.

But when you love someone

You just don't treat them bad

Oh, how I feel so sad now that I wanna leave...

She grabbed the remote and hit mute. "Let me find out. What you know about Donnel Jones?"

"I like that song right there. My mother was big on R&B so that's pretty much all we listened to. She hated when I put on rap music." Mox laughed at the memory.

"That's cool," She said. "So, that's *two* things we have in common."

"What's the first?"

"Our love for cars."

"Oh, yeah... definitely." Mox looked over the warm, plush apartment. It was nicely furnished and laced with wall to wall carpet, a brown micro fiber sectional couch with matching love seat and a big screen floor unit television. "Damn, you look good."

Priscilla blushed. "Thank you." She was really feeling Mox's air. He was unique in a way she couldn't describe, extremely mature and incomparable; a far cry from the ordinary.

Mox spread his arms and went to hug Priscilla.

She had to get on her tippy toes just to wrap her arms around his neck, she was 5'7, but Mox was two inches over six feet.

She looked good rocking a pair of off white linen shorts, a pink tank-top and a pair of white, ankle strap Louis Vuitton heels. The perfume she wore was seductive and sweet.

Her soft breasts pressed against Mox's chest and he wrapped his arms around her curvy waist.

After their embrace, Mox went to take a seat on the couch.

"You live here by yourself?" He asked.

"Yup."

"Wassup wit' your parents?"

Priscilla didn't mind sharing her personal issues with Mox. It was confusing, but she was comfortable with it.

She sat down on the couch beside him and took a deep breath. "Well, my father..." She paused and looked to the ceiling. It was a touchy subject. "I don't even know. As far as I'm concerned, I don't have a father."

"Nah, don't say that. I mean, he's still alive right?"

"I guess so."

Mox could tell it was difficult for her to explain the situation. He had been going through the same issues with his expression of the traumatic incident in his life, but the more he spoke about it the better he handled it.

"I'm being nosy but, what about your mother?"

The matters of her and her mother's affairs were far more sensitive to discuss than the absence of her father. Priscilla slighted her mother for reasons she withheld from the world, but you could see the affliction in her eyes when it was mentioned.

All she said was, “She’s around.”

Mox didn’t want to force her to talk about it. “Okay. That’s good. At least you still have them.”

“They’re both dead to me.”

He wasn’t too fond of that statement. “That aint cool Priscilla. Please don’t say things like that around me.”

She was rattled by his remark. “Oh, really? Huh...” She turned her lip up. “Well, what’s your story, Mr. Daniels? You can’t be the only one asking questions. First of all what color are your eyes? I never seen anybody with eyes that color and what about you mother and father?”

“My eye color is called true amber. I really don’t know too much about how and why I have them, but I do know that they’re very rare.” Mox took a breather and relaxed back on the velvety cushion. He closed his eyes. “As far as my parents...they’re dead.”

A mini smiled appeared on Priscilla’s face and was immediately gone once she understood he wasn’t playing.

"You're not joking, are you?"

He opened his eyes and sat up. "I don't joke about shit like that. That's why I asked you not to say what you said." Mox stood up and walked to the window that overlooked Pelham Road. "You should be grateful that both your parents are still here. Never take that for granted because when they do go... it's over. You don't get anymore." He turned and looked at Priscilla. "I wish I could bring my parents *back*."

Before she became too emotional, Priscilla stood and went over to Mox. "I'm sorry. I didn't mean to—"

He interrupted her and placed his index finger to his lips. "Shh... I'm good, don't worry about it."

"When did this happen?"

"Five years ago."

Priscilla was taken aback. She couldn't comprehend how a person who lost both parents only five years ago was so poised and level headed.

"That shit don't fuck wit' your head?"

"Hell yeah; every day... I try to block it out, but the fact is, the person who killed them is still on the streets and that bothers me."

"That's crazy." She said, returning to the kitchen. "Excuse my poor hospitality, would you like something to drink?"

"Sure. A glass of water is cool." Priscilla poured two glasses of water and sat back on the couch. "Now, enough with the formalities; wassup wit' this sixty-thousand in one night?"

She laughed. "I knew that was coming sooner or later. Come here, sit down." Mox took his seat next to Priscilla. "I'ma be straight forward with you, I'm usually not this open to people about my personal business, but I like you and I see you've got potential."

"Oh yeah, thank you."

"You're welcome, but for real... you know you can have anything in the world you desire... all you gotta do is believe in it and work hard to achieve it. The boundaries are limitless." Priscilla sipped her water. "This time last year, I was homeless, dead broke and on the verge of a nervous breakdown until I met someone who changed my life. His name is Juan Carlos Ortega and he's a Columbian drug lord. I'm not gonna lie, at first our relationship was physical, but after things didn't work out, we continued to have a business relationship."

Mox was thrown off. "Why you tellin' me this?"

"Because, Mox. This man will give me anything I want. He already gave me another opportunity at life and now it's my turn to give someone else a chance to live out their dreams."

He still didn't fully comprehend where she was going with the conversation.

"Are you serious, or is this some type joke?"

"No, I'm serious... look." She got up from the couch and went into the back room. When she returned she was holding a brown shopping bag. She placed it on the black and white, marble top coffee table. "Open the bag." She said.

Mox peeled the bag open, reached inside and grabbed the contents out. He placed the two, taped up, rectangular packages on the table.

"What the fuck is this?" He asked.

"What does it look like?"

He grinned. “Look like cocaine to me.”

“Excactly.”

“You got it all wrong if you think you gon’ have me out on some corner slangin’ ten and twenty dollar bags of coke. Not gonna happen.” He stood up like he was about to leave.

Priscilla grabbed his arm. “That’s not what I think, just sit down and let me explain it to you. It won’t take long and if you don’t agree, then you can leave, no love lost.”

He sat down and finished the rest of his water. “I’m listening.” He said.

“One of these,” She touched the package. “go for twenty-five thousand dollars in the streets. I get them wholesale from Juan Carlos for only ten thousand; therefore, the profit on each one is fifteen thousand. I’m willing to split the fifteen in half with you if you help me move them.”

“Help you?”

“Yes.”

“And how am I supposed to do that? Priscilla, I aint never sold drugs a day in my life. I wouldn’t know where to begin.”

"This is why I'm here, Mox. I'm gonna show you everything you need to know and I guarantee you in a month's time your whole life will be different. All you gotta do is follow my lead."

Priscilla's verbal abilities were immaculate. She could broker a million dollar drug deal and in the same sentence, turn around and slick talk her way out of trouble. It was gift that God had given her and she had Mox hypnotized within minutes, but the crazy part was; her feelings for him were heartfelt and genuine.

"What about your boy, Deandre?"

"Listen Mox, the only reason I fuck with Deandre is because his sister and I are real close. She asked me to put him on so he could help out with their bills and that's what I did, but he ain't you Mox. They only reason he's in that position is because I put him there." she rose from her seat and faced Mox. "These niggas out here don't want nothing but a few thousand in their pocket to front with, some new sneakers and a bunch clothes. I know you want more outta life than that Mox."

They eyed each other steadily. The chemistry was evident and highly explosive. Mox didn't have to say a word; she already knew what he wanted.

"And you ride around in the car with him *because?*"

"Because, he can't be trusted and he doesn't have a business mind. If I give him something I ride around with him until he finishes it. I take my cut and I go, but all that comes to an end the second you tell me yes."
Mox took a minute to process everything Priscilla was speaking on. This type of opportunity didn't present itself on an everyday basis. It was two choices he had; struggle and hope things eventually get better or take action and make an immediate change.

"So how's this supposed to work?"

They smiled at each other and then Priscilla instructed him on everything he needed to do.

November, 2001

Mox was beginning to establish himself as one of the main suppliers of cocaine in Westchester County and he managed to stay under the radar because he was smart and he knew how to move.

He hadn't bought a car yet, he didn't wear jewelry and he was still living in his Aunt's apartment in the projects, but on occasion he would spend the night with Priscilla.

Their mental and physical bond was amplified and Mox's feelings were as strong as he had ever known them to be for a woman other than his mother. Over a year's time, they formed an allegiance on respect, honor and trust. They even came up with a mantra and had it tattooed in the same spot behind their ear. It read; *Let no-one stand before WE* and it was written in script with blood red ink.

Mox was 16 years old and in love with a woman that was three years older. At least he felt like he was. He had never known the true meaning of love, but when Priscilla was in his presence he experienced completion; it was as if she could almost fill the void of his mother in an odd kind of way.

After the two most important people in his life were taken away so abruptly, Mox pledged to himself that the next person to touch something he loved would die. And his word was bond.

The day Mox accepted Priscilla's offering is the same day she cut all ties to Deandre. Of course he had no idea why she so abruptly stop coming around, but the word would soon hit the wind like a hustler with poor quality work and he would find out that *Mox* was now the one in power.

The unexpected shift in ranking was something that Deandre didn't think too highly of. In fact, he was ready to do something extreme; and he did.

The entire day had been tranquil and stagnant. Mox lazed in his boxers on the spongy sofa in Priscilla's living room, punching buttons on the remote control. He was looking for the History channel. It was Tuesday, his day off and he was waiting for her to come back from food shopping.

The house phone rang, Mox leaned up and stared at it lying on the table in front of him. He let it ring until it stopped.

He *never* answered Priscilla's phone. If it was her, she would call his cell phone.

As soon as he went to lie back, his cell phone rang.

He ruffled through some papers, saw Priscilla's name on the caller ID and fumbled to get it open.

"Hello?"

"Wassup you bitchassnigga!" The caller laughed loudly.

Mox thought it was a joke. "Yo, stop playing on the phone. Where my girl at?"

"Shut the fuck up and listen! I got yo bitch, nigga... and if you wanna see her lil' pretty fuckin' ass again, I'ma need you to go get a bag, put a hunit thousand cash in it and wait for me to call this number back in twelve hours, ya dig?"

Mox took the phone off his ear and looked at the screen a second time. It did say Priscilla. He got up from the couch and went to look out the living room window.

"Who the fuck is this?"

"Oh, you think it's a joke nigga..." He slammed the phone down on a table and Mox pressed the speaker to his ear so he could hear better. He could only make out some rustling and the sound of a wooden chair being dragged across the floor.

The caller's voice was getting louder. "Hurry up nigga, bring that bitch over here!" He picked the phone back up. "You think I'm playing, nigga! I got somebody wanna holla at you."

A scream came from the other end. "Hellllppp!" Mox's eyes lit up.

"Shut up bitch!" You heard the slap of his hand hitting someone's flesh. "Say hi to your little boyfriend." He put the phone to her face.

"Mox help me, please???" Priscilla cried.

Deandre snatched the phone back. "A hunit thousand nigga! Twelve hours!" Then he clicked.

Mox dropped the phone and pressed his temples with the palm of his hand. "Arrhhh!" He belted.

When Wise Earl found out his nephew was hustling and then witnessed for himself, the magnitude in which he did it, all he could do was offer his prudent knowledge to the young hustler on the come up. He warned Mox,

If you in this game for the sole purpose of getting rich, then you gon' have to forget about anything you love. Because the second a nigga see you got love in your heart for something, they gon' try to take it away from you.

At that precise moment, Mox could hear his uncle's sharp, raspy voice vibrating in his ear, repeating those exact words.

He was nervous, his hands were shaky and he was pacing back and forth. *Calm down Mox!* He inhaled a breath of the cool central air that flowed through the apartment and closed his eyes. He tried counting to ten like he had seen someone do in a movie, but every time he got to four his concentration would shift.

Mox hurried to the back room and threw on a hoodie and some sweatpants. He opened the large closet at the back of Priscilla's room, slipped into a pair of sneakers and grabbed the Northface book bag that was buried in the corner.

The worriment was swelling and his thoughts were wondering.

I hope they didn't touch her?

What if I give these niggas the money and they still kill her?

"Fuck!" He tossed the bag onto the queen sized bed and stood at the foot with both hands over his face. His breathing was heavy. He silently prayed and asked God;

Why?

Mox bent down, unzipped the bag and started pulling stacks of money out. Once he reached ten, he closed the bag up and went back into the living room.

Paying the $100,000 ransom wasn't a problem or a second thought. If that's what it took to get Priscilla back, it was a small price to pay.

He searched the table and the couch for his phone before spotting it on the floor by the window. When he picked it up he saw a missed call from Javier, his co-worker/Lieutenant.

A thought stumbled into Mox's brain and he quickly cooked up a scheme, but he needed help. He pressed the seven numbers into his phone.

It rang two times and Javier picked up. "Mox, I was callin..."

He cut in. "Javier, I need your help."

"Yeah, anything Mox... you alright?"

"I... I can't talk over the phone. I'm on my way to you," he stuttered.

"Aight, I'm here."

Mox went to the kitchen and got the keys to Priscilla's other car. He snatched the book bag and went to meet up with Javier.

Eleven hours and fifty-five minutes later, Mox's cell phone rang. He looked around the room and then he answered it.

"Hello?"

"You got that?"

"Yeah."

Mox envisioned Deandre smiling ear to ear smile.

"Aight, this is what it is... I want you to—"

He broke in. "Hold up, homie..." the phone went silent for a few seconds and then Mox picked it back up. " I got somebody wanna holla at you."

"Deandre, please... let that girl go!" his mother cried. "They gon' kill us!"

He couldn't believe what he was hearing.

Mrs. Foster and his little sister, Shelly, were tied up to two chairs with their wrist and ankles duct taped, confined to a soggy, dark room that reeked of urine.

Tears covered their faces, but they kept their eyes on Javier and his two Mexican comrades that were off to the left holding fully automatic weapons.

"Deandre, you there?"

"Yo, I swear to God, Mox... if you touch my mother or my little sister, I'ma fuckin' kill you."

"You *still* makin' threats?" Mox put the phone directly in front of his mouth. "I got your mother and your little sister over here duct taped and tied up. I'm 'bout to flip a coin. Yeah, read between the lines, nigga. Now this is how we gon' do it... give Priscilla that phone and when she calls me and tells me she's safe, I'll let your people go."

Deandre shot back. "I don't trust you."

"You got no choice." He clicked.

Twenty minutes later, Priscilla called Mox and let him know that she made it home safe.

He released the Foster family without harm. Two weeks later police found Deandre dead in his car, parked in the back of the Stop & Shop Supermarket on Palmer Avenue. He suffered two gunshot wounds to the head.

Following the Foster boy's murder, Mox could no longer duck in the shadows and creep below the radar; he was on front-street now. The whole city knew about it, but the police didn't have enough evidence to charge him and he was fully aware of that.

Right after he killed Deandre, Mox went back to Priscilla's to shower and go to sleep.

No nightmares.

No visions.

Not even a thought about it, but his whole world changed after that.

THREE

A slight glare from the sun's rays squinted through a crack in the window shade as Mox sat at the foot end of his twin sized bed finishing off a second bowl of cinnamon toast crunch. His attention was on the exclusive news flash that came across the 32 inch screen in front of him.

It had been ten months since the World Trade Center bombing and the magnitude of destruction was still inconceivable. He watched as video recordings played back the frightening incident that touched the world. All of his thoughts were on all the families that suffered the loss of a loved one and how their lives were abruptly transformed within minutes and he could identify with them. He felt the same pain they did.

The fateful loss of his parents was still fresh on his brain and the only way to cease the reoccurring visions was to find out the truth.

Mox placed the empty cereal bowl on top of the television and looked down at Priscilla while she slept, peacefully. Reaching down, he tugged lightly on the bed sheets exposing her nudeness. Her skin was flawless; like an airbrushed model in a print magazine, delicate; like an invaluable piece of art; and extremely enticing.

Mox crawled into bed behind Priscilla and inhaled her sweet essence. The pleasurable aroma got him excited and his manhood began to pulsate. It escaped through the slit in his boxer shorts and tickled her ass cheek. He reached around, put his hand between her warm, moist thighs and let his middle finger slip into her kitten.

Priscilla moaned.

Seconds later, her love syrup dribbled down Mox's knuckle.

She reached back and caressed his hardened manhood and whispered. "Get a condom."

Mox rolled onto his back and snatched a condom off the small, wooden nightstand. It was out the wrapper and on his dick in one breath.

He shoved himself halfway inside of her.

Priscilla's walls tightened and she squeezed his muscle.

Mox went deeper.

"Oohh... Mox."

He held her shoulder with his left hand and gripped her waistline with his right. The speed of his stroke increased by the seconds and the slapping sound of her soft ass cheeks against his well sculpted thighs grew louder.

Priscilla buried her face in the pillow and continued moving in rhythmic motion. Grunts of pleasure escaped her lips and she climaxed for the second time.

"Yes, Mox! Fuck me!"

Her assertive sex talk always turned him on.

Mox flipped her onto her stomach and proceeded to thrust himself deep inside of her until he reached his peak.

They rolled over, exhausted, sweaty and out of breath.

Priscilla looked in Mox's eyes. She wiped the sweat from his forehead and kissed his lips.

“What’s wrong?” She questioned, noticing his mind was someplace else.

The expression on his face was silent and his eyes held a puzzled stare.

“Nothing, why you ask?”

Priscilla sat up in the bed. “Because Mox, we just finishing fuckin’ and now you act like you do want me to touch you.”

“It’s not that Priscilla.”

“Well, what is it?”

Mox rubbed his shiny bald head, pondering. “It’s this whole situation with my parents—it ain’t adding up to me, things don’t feel right.”

“Mox, listen.” Priscilla got up, walked around the bed and sat on his lap. “I understand how you’re feeling, but you can’t let this control your life.”

The frustration in the pit of his soul was boiling. Priscilla had no idea what it was like to wake up to a bloodbath. To watch your parents, especially your mother, take her last breaths in front of you. Maybe she did go through a few things, who hasn't? But whatever her troubles were, they had no similarities to Mox's experience.

"Stop comparing your situation to mine," Mox moved Priscilla off his lap and got up. "It's different, you still got your mother; she's alive."

"Mox, you know I don't fuck wit' my moms."

"That's because you choose not to. I never had a choice... this shit was cast upon me like a death ridden plague."

"So, what are you gonna do?"

He picked a towel up and tossed it to Priscilla. "I'ma do whatever I need to do to fix it. Take a shower and get dressed... we going for a ride."

An hour later Mox pulled the polished Mercedes to the curb at the corner of 241st and White Plains Road in the Bronx.

As soon as he turned the corner the area became familiar. His recollection was detailed and vivid, as if a mental picture was embedded in his brain.

His thoughts took him back twelve years and he could see his mother's 1988 burgundy Nissan Stanza with the one hubcap, a blown out passenger side window that was filled in with a garbage bag and malfunctioning brake lights.

That was her baby, as she called it.

Priscilla tapped Mox's shoulder breaking his concentration. "Why did you pull over?"

He took the key out the ignition and let his head fall back onto the headrest. "When I was younger my mother use to move around a lot and I was with her most of the time, whether she was going to get drugs or we were going to church... I was right by her side. I saw plenty of things I probably shouldn't have seen, Priscilla, but at the end of the day those experiences shaped my way of thinking and forced me to become very observant."

Priscilla thought about her own trials as a child and how her mother was the total opposite. She admired Wanda's attempt to be in Mox's life, unlike her mother, who was always quick to chastise and humiliate her every opportunity she got.

"There are things a child's eyes shouldn't see." She said.

Mox looked into the rearview mirror. "Well, my eyes seen it all."

"Nobody would watch you for her?"

"The only person she trusted to watch over me was my aunt Sybil and she worked a lot, so I *had* to be with her, and then she had Casey and it was all three of us running around in these streets." Mox opened his wallet, pulled out a picture and stared at it. "We would travel all over New York... that's how I learned the highways and all the major streets in the five boroughs." It was a photo of him, Casey and his mother in front of Rockefeller Center.

"Can I see?" Priscilla asked, reaching for the picture.

Mox handed it to her.

"Wow," She smiled. "You and Casey look just like your mother."

The brothers shared a lot of the same features as their mother, from their dark skin tone and structure of their faces to the size and shaping of their lips and ears.

"Everybody says that."

"If you don't mind me asking, where was your father?" She handed the photo back.

“That nigga only came around when he felt it was necessary. If my mother didn’t have no money, he didn’t wanna be bothered with us.”

“That’s crazy.”

“Not really.” He said. “The whole time I knew him I never felt that father and son bond between us, so his absence didn’t really bother me. It might sound a little awkward, but that’s what it was.”

A silence settled in and for a few seconds they sat staring into the sky, listening to the sound of passing cars.

Priscilla finally spoke. “So, why are we here?”

“Because I keep gettin’ a vision of this store every time I close my eyes,” Mox smirked. “My mother loved to smoke weed. I remember her bringing me here all the time. We would go to the store over there,” He pointed across the street. “And she would get whatever she needed to get and then we left... I’m hoping one of these dudes can lead me to some information. Maybe somebody in there knows her.”

“Mox, that was more than seven years ago. Do you think the same people still work there?”

He pushed the car door open. “I don’t know, but I’m ‘bout to find out. Come get in the driver’s seat and start the car up.”

“You don’t want me to come with you?”

“Naw, I need you in the car in case something happen and we gotta get outta here.”

Priscilla sat behind the wheel and watched Mox walk across the street. He got to the door, pushed it open and entered.

The inside of the store was just the way he remembered it; cluttered, dimly lit and clouded with smoke from the incense that burned all day. The shelves were over packed with early dated vinyl records and up to date reggae CD’s.

A tall, brown skinned man with a ragged beard and thick, long, golden dread locks stood behind the cash register.

Mox approached the counter, his ears filled with Peter Tosh’s tranquilizing vocals as he sang through the speakers, *Wanted Dred & Alive*.

“Yes, young one... how can mi help you today?” His accent, strong, but clear enough to understand.

Mox focused his eyes on a painting that covered the back wall. It was a picture of a fair skinned man in a suit with a chiseled face, curly hair and a bunch of medals on his lapel. He was sitting at a table.

"Who is that?" He asked.

"Dat's Haile Selassie I... him da emperor of E-t-opia fa four decades!" He lifted his right hand and held up four fingers. "He da reincarnation of Jesus Christ, bredren... him gon' leed us to Zion!"

Mox felt the passion and reverence in his every word. He extended his arm and they shook hands.

"My name is Mox."

"Mox, eh... dat's a very distinctive name, bredren." He turned and called out to someone in the back. "Tyga!"

"Yah!?" They yelled back.

"Come to de front!... sorry bredren, mi name Lion." He eyed Mox. "You look familiar bredren, you from ear?"

"Naw, not really." He said, reaching into his pocket. "I got another question though." Mox placed the picture on top of the counter. "You know her?"

Lion picked the photo up and looked at it closely. He pulled out a pair of rim wire glasses from the front pocket of his shirt and fixed them on his face.

"Bloodclaaat!" He screamed, throwing his hands to the sky. "Tyga, come now!"

"So, you know her?"

Lion sucked his teeth and slowly removed the glasses from his face. Within seconds, his entire demeanor had switched.

A short, dark, broad shouldered Rasta with dreadlocks stumbled out the back room gripping a black 500 Mossberg pump at his waistline.

"Mox meet Tyga, him a shotta! Now you gwan hafta tell mi a lickle more 'bout why you ear..."

Mox remained calm. "I told you why I was here. That's my mother in that picture."

Lion turned and held the picture up to show Tyga.

"Dat's da dead boy Reginald woman." Tyga growled.

Mox stared at the husky man holding the shotgun. "Yeah, I'm Reginald's son."

Lion whipped his thick, golden locks around and faced Mox. "Reginald your father?"

"Yup."

"Well, mi do a favor for Reginald; a fifteen tousand dolla favor... and him never pay me back."

Mox shook his head. He knew where this was going.

"I'm sorry to hear that dred, but he's dead now."

"Yes," Lion chuckled. "Mi know him dead, but since him your father... now *you* owe me his det!"

Tyga rushed around the counter and put the barrel of the shotgun to Mox's stomach.

The front door swung open and the nozzle of a double action, black polymer .9 millimeter Baby Eagle was the first thing visible.

"Drop that shit slowly or they gon' be sweeping them nasty ass dreds off the floor."

"Tyga!" Lion shouted. "Gun 'em!"

"Shit!" Mox cursed. "Priscilla, I told you to stay in the car."

"Seven minutes Mox. You know the rules." She clenched the baby cannon with two hands, her eyes, focused on the shotgun toting Rasta.

Tyga lowered the weapon, finally dropping it to the floor.

Lion took a step back and raised his hands to the sky. "Mi naw want no problem, bredren."

"I don't want no problems either Dred, I just want some answers." Mox stated. "I need to know who my mother and father were dealing with... anybody they associated with."

Lion's eyes shifted to the barrel of the pistol. "Mi nah know a ting, bredren." He lied.

Mox bent down to pick the shotgun up. "I think you lying to me dred."

"Pussyhole... mi nah lie."

"You like sports, Dred?" Mox grabbed the nozzle of the Mossberg and handled the 30 inch pump like a baseball bat.

Lion ignored him, sucked his teeth and then shot Tyga a distasteful glare.

"I love me some baseball..." Mox continued. "Last year I was All American, ranked number six in the country. They called me, M. Daniels." Mox positioned himself like he was at the plate, ready to take a pitch. "It didn't matter if the pitcher could throw ninety five miles per hour..." He raised the shotgun and twirled it like he was about to swing for the fence. "I was tay-king-it-out-the park!" Aiming for his ribs, Mox swung the lightweight weapon with as much strength as he could muster.

The force of the blow shattered Lion's elbow when he tried to block it and he collapsed to the floor.

Again, Mox swung, this time slamming the weapon down on his leg, crushing bones on impact.

Lion writhed in pain, but somehow managed to not scream.

"Hol lon!" Tyga reasoned. He wanted to help. "Mi tell you, mi tell you."

Mox moved toward Tyga. "See, now he's a real friend."

"Tyga, ya nah gwan tell dis faassie boy nuttin'." Lion was furious.

"Yo," Mox nodded at Priscilla. "Shut him up."

Priscilla pressed the cold steel to Lion's lips. "All I need is a reason." She whispered.

It wasn't the first time she had held a gun to someone's head and it sure wouldn't be the last.

"Tyga, tell me something before this shit get crazy." Mox cautioned.

Tyga's lip quivered, he was timorous. In all the years he had stood by Lion's side never once had he seen him get treated this way. People feared Lion.

"All mi kno is..." He looked at his helpless friend. "Reginald use to work for de white man, dey call him The Ghost."

"The Ghost? Why they call him that?"

"Because, afta him murder ya whole family—" He paused and looked Mox in his eyes. "Him vanish!"

Mox wasn't at all moved by Tyga's story. "That's it? Where can I find this Ghost?"

Tyga shook his head slowly and a demonic grin appeared on his face. "Ya nah gwan find him… him gwan find you!"

Mox was angry, and when he became angry his inner beast would rear its hideous face. It was like a Dr. Jekyl and Mr. Hyde transformation. One minute he was calm, restrained and well mannered, and then, at the blink of an eye he could become violent, audacious and discourteous.

He could never figure out where this maniacal being derived from, but at times he enjoyed it; it was gratifying. He was able to unshackle those locked up feelings and set them free.

"Go start the car." He hadn't looked at her or said her name, but Priscilla knew it was time to go. She backed away from Lion and stepped out the door.

Mox ordered Tyga to sit on the floor next to Lion.

"I need to get a message to this Ghost guy, who's gon' deliver it?" Tyga slightly raised his hand and nodded his head. "Good… so we don't need him." He lifted the black 500 and let it explode.

The roaring blast was ear-piercing and the slug blew away the top half of Lion's head. Blood, brains and dredlocks were everywhere. "Tell The Ghost we need to speak."

Before Mox left the small store, he checked the back room and came out with a Puma duffle bag containing three pounds of high grade marijuana and $65,000 cash.

He wiped the shotgun of his prints, snatched the photo off the counter and walked away from the scene with no regret.

When he got to the car, he tossed the bag into the backseat and jumped in the passenger. The first thing he said was, "Where you get that gun from, Priscilla?"

"Damn, can I pull off?" She put the car in drive and sped away. "I took it from my brother."

Mox reclined his seat. "You know you could'a got me killed back there."

"I was just tryna help."

"I'm sure you were, but if you listen to me... that would be an even bigger help."

Priscilla cut her eyes at Mox. "I can handle myself."

Mox laughed and they rode in silence the rest of the way back.

FOUR

November 2003

Mox was still working at the car wash, the only difference now was that he controlled a $200,000 a-week cocaine operation and Shiny Gleam was his headquarters.

As soon as he was put into position, Mox recruited all five of his co-workers and appointed them each a specific job. All he did is answer his phone and count the money. He hadn't touched drugs since the day Priscilla presented the offer to him and that's how he liked it.

The dealings were run so precisely that it never interfered with the daily car wash flow. Nobody saw drugs come in and nobody saw them go out.

At the least, Mox would move 7-10 kilo's a week, sometimes 15, but if he really wanted to turn it up, he could easily move 20-30 without breaking a sweat.

Priscilla had customers coming in from out of town on a daily basis. It was no longer unusual to see out of state plates pulling into the Shiny Gleam and some days the parking lot resembled a car show, but the supervisors never knew a thing because all the drug flow did was enhance the already profitable business.

Everything Priscilla said to Mox eventually came to fruition. He was young, black, handsome and rich, living a lifestyle most people dreamt about, but he was never content.

Being a drug dealer was never in his plans. In the beginning, all he wanted to do was find the man that murdered his parents. Somewhere down the line he got sidetracked and lost focus.

Not a bit of information on "The Ghost" had surfaced since the record shop murder and Mox didn't have any other leads to go on. A few times he even felt like giving up, but seeing that picture in his wallet always reassured him that he was fighting for something that meant a lot to him. At any cost he was going to find who he was looking for.

When Mox first asked Priscilla if he would have to kill anybody for the money, her response was, *only if you want to.*

After a year in the game he learned that meant; *of course you are.*

The feeling Mox got after he killed Lion was nothing compared to what he felt when he murdered Deandre.

FIVE

February 2004

Mox came to a stop at the red light at Lincoln and North Avenue. He looked up in the rearview mirror and saw a blue and white NRPD patrol car slowing up behind him. He snatched the seatbelt and quickly snapped it in. When the light turned green he made the right and went up North Avenue with the patrol car following.

As soon as he passed the bus depot the cop tossed his lights on.

"Fuck!" He cursed aloud seeing the flashing red lights in his mirror. Mox didn't know why he was being flagged, he had his seatbelt on and he was doing the speed limit.

He pulled the $90,000 Aston Martin to the curb and waited for the officer. When he heard the cop's voice come through the horn, that's when he got nervous.

"Driver! Let me see your hands!"

Mox shut the ignition off and placed both of his hands outside the window.

Two more patrol cars and an unmarked had arrived on the scene.

At 12:10 in the afternoon on a Wednesday, in the middle of North Avenue, in the blistering cold, the New Rochelle police department had Mox Daniels surrounded and he didn't even know what he did.

Pedestrians looked on in astonishment as two officers ran at the car from opposite angles with their guns drawn. One of them snatched the door open and yanked Mox from the driver's seat.

"Yo, what the fuc—"

In two seconds, Mox was faced down on the frosted pavement with a knee in his back and a .40 Caliber to his head.

"New Rochelle police, don't fuckin' move!" He screamed in Mox's ear.

A short, black detective with a terrible receding hairline stepped in.

"Bring 'em up." He told them.

They brought Mox to his feet.

He had tiny pieces of gravel stuck to the left side of his cheek from his face being pressed against the cold concrete and one of his sneakers had come off.

"Mox Daniels, you're under arrest for the murder of Deandre Foster. At this time anything you say can and will be used against you in a court of law. You—"

Mox went completely deaf for a few seconds. He stared directly at the detective, watching his mouth move, but no sound came out.

One officer shouted. "We got something!" and lifted a black .9 millimeter out the glove compartment.

Mox turned, saw the officer holding the gun up and shook his head.

Priscilla.

He was arraigned on murder and gun charges and then two days later a judge set bail at one million dollars.

County Jail - Valhalla, New York

(Visiting Room)

After a thirty-five minute drive and standing in line for over an hour, Priscilla finally made it to the inside of the visiting area of the county jail. She went through the search, gave the C.O. her slip and was escorted to a table in the far left corner of the room.

It was her first time coming to visit anyone in prison, so she was amazed at how many women came to see their boyfriends, husbands, and family members. What she didn't like was people searching through her shit. Once she got past that, she was good.

As she scanned the room, she counted thirty tables and every one of them was occupied. Every few minutes, an inmate and his/her visitors would depart and go their separate ways and two minutes later, more visitors and another inmate would be at the table.

Mox came through the door, passed the guard a piece of paper and was directed to his table.

She got up when she saw him walking toward her and they hugged.

Mox embraced her firmly, but not too hard. He rested his face in the nape of her neck and kissed her gently and then moved to her lips. Their tongues twisted, and before they broke away, Priscilla slipped something down Mox's pants.

"Damn..." She said, savoring the taste of his saliva. She pecked his lips once more before she sat down. "That suit is real bright." She tugged at his orange county jumpsuit.

Mox smirked. "Oh, you got jokes, huh?"

Priscilla blushed. She almost couldn't look him in his eyes. She felt guilty.

"I'm sorry Mox."

He clenched his teeth. "I told you about that fuckin' gun Priscilla."

"I know Mox, I'm sorry," water built up in her eyes. She sniffled and wiped them away. She had been careless and left her gun in his car.

"Listen baby, don't cry..." He grabbed Priscilla's hands and held them tight. "I'm just a little upset right now and I don't mean to take it out on you. Don't worry about this... all this shit gon' go away."

"What are they saying?"

"They aint saying nothing. That murder charge is bullshit; I can beat that with the right lawyer." He looked around and lowered his tone. "But this other thing might sit me down for a sec."

"How long is a second, Mox?"

"It all depends. Did you do what I asked you to do?"

Priscilla didn't even hear the question, she was too busy watching the man to the right of them ice grill Mox.

She whispered. "Why he looking at you like that?"

Mox glanced and smirked. "That's Deandre's little cousin, Rudy. I think he wants revenge." he laughed.

"That's not funny Mox. You better be careful in here."

"I got him taken care of. That's why I told you to bring this." He pointed to his pants. "So, what did he say?"

"Who?"

"Juan Carlos, Priscilla."

She got lost for a minute. "Oh, he said if he does this for you, you're gonna have to owe him a favor."

Mox rubbed his head. "I figured that. Tell him everything is good. Just hurry up." he leaned in to kiss her lips. "Damn, you taste good."

Priscilla couldn't help but smile. It had only been two days and she was missing her man crazily.

The one hour visit had gone by quickly.

"Daniels, time's up." The guard came to the table and handed Mox his pass.

"Okay, a few days and you should be out of here." She kissed him one more time before she turned to leave. "I love you."

It was the first time she said it and it caught Mox off guard. He didn't know what to say back even though he had the same feeling, so he said nothing and let her walk through the doors.

"Daniels, let's go!" The guard shouted again.

Mox was housed in a part of the prison that they called "The Old Jail" specifically because of the old, rusted bars, molded and cracked walls and no hot water. In the summertime, the walls would sweat and in the winter they would be ice blocks, literally. It was just like the jails you see in those old movies; 23 hour lockdown with one hour of rec.

As soon as he got back to his cell, Mox put a sheet up and stripped to his boxers. He reached into the briefs he had on underneath and pulled out two balloons the same length and width as his thumb. He bit the small knots at the top and ripped the latex apart.

The C.O's keys were jingling and Mox knew he was getting closer to his cell. He stashed the ripped balloons and the contents under the thin, county issued mattress and sat on the toilet.

"What the fuck you in there doin' inmate!?" The C.O pulled the sheet back and peeked in.

Mox had a magazine in his hand, sitting on the toilet with his draws on his ankles. "Taking a shit, C.O."

He Looked at Mox and turned his nose up. "You gonna fuckin' stink the joint up, inmate. Put some fuckin' water on that shit... and hurry up and get this sheet off my goddamn bars." He let go of the sheet, walked back down the tier and hollered. *"Count in five minutes, ladies!"*

Mox jumped up and pushed the weak mattress to the side. He tossed the ripped balloons in the toilet, flushed them and unrolled the five one-hundred dollar bills Priscilla had given him. The other balloon was full of marijuana.

Getting the contraband into the prison was an easy task for Mox because he knew one of the visiting room C.O's. Usually after a visit you had to walk through a metal detector and get stripped searched before going back to your block, but because Mox had a name and he was able to dish out a few dead presidents; he was invisible to the guards.

He peeled off two big faces, folded them up as small as he could and then he threw his orange county pants back on and snatched the sheet off the bars. Before the guard called the count, Mox rolled up a couple of sticks, scribbled something on a piece of paper and sent the note two cells down on a line.

"On the count!" The C.O hollered.

Mox stood at the entrance of his cell and waited for the guard to make his round.

"Williams!" The guard shouted into the cell next to Mox. *"Williams, get your ass on the gate! It's count time."*

When they called count you had to be on your feet, standing at your gate in full county oranges and there was absolutely no talking.

An hour and a half passed, count cleared and the shift changed.

Mox hopped off his bunk once he heard the C.O call out, *"On the chow!"*

He stood by his gate and waited for the trustee to come by.

"Yo, wassup?" He stopped at Mox's cell. He was a chubby, light skinned kid with corn row braids. "That was you who sent the kite, right?" he slid Mox's food tray through the feed up in the bars.

Mox spoke low. "Yeah… your name Botta Bing, right?"

"Yeah… why?"

"Nah, my boy Javier told me that you and him is good. He said you could get me what I needed. " Mox flashed a few of the rollies he had in his hand.

"Oh, yeah…" Botta Bing nodded. "Yeah, I got that kite. What's the situation though?"

Mox stuffed three rollies and the two hundred dollars into his hand. "I need what's on that paper tomorrow morning, and then at lunch I need you to bring 4 cell's tray over here before you give it to him."

Botta Bing screwed his face up. "That's askin' a lot." he looked down at what Mox had given him. "I'm sayin' that's the nigga Rudy's cell, right? Check it," he looked down the tier. "I don't like that nigga anyway, so whatever problems yall got, that's between yall. I'm just sayin'" he shrugged his broad shoulders and made a gesture with his hands. "You don't know me, I don't know you."

Mox smiled. “Exactly.”

The next morning Botta Bing tapped on Mox’s cell and slid his breakfast tray through the feed up.

Mox got up and went to the gate. “Did you get it?”

Botta Bing passed him a small, plastic tube that looked like perfume. “Yo, what the fuck is that shit?”

“Ebony Dream.” Mox grinned. “Make sure you bring that tray over here at lunch.”

Later that afternoon Rudy Foster had to be rushed across the street to Westchester Medical Center to get his stomach pumped, but the doctors couldn’t figure out what caused it.

The following day Mox made bail and walked out of the county jail a free man.

As soon as he stepped into the parking lot, a black guy in a grey suit approached him. “Mr. Daniels,” he called out.

Mox kept walking. He sped his pace up. If it was the feds, they were going to have to wrestle him down.

The black guy in the suit called again. “Mr. Daniels, I’m a friend of Juan Carlos.”

Mox stopped and turned around. “Who?”

“Juan Carlos.” He gave Mox his card. “I just spoke with Priscilla. She told me to meet you here. My name is Charles Woods and I’ll be representing you throughout this process.”

Mox took the card and looked it over. “Where my girl at?”

“I told her we had a few things to discuss about your case, so she went home to wait for you.”

“Aint nothing to discuss.” Mox started to walk off.

Charles pulled a manila folder from his briefcase and tapped Mox on his arm with it. “Somebody was there Mox.”

He spun his neck around quickly. “I don’t know what the fuck you talking about. Nobody was no-where.”

Charles opened the folder and handed Mox a photo of a young white kid with dirty blonde hair, blue eyes and a few freckles on his nose. “Billy Worsham; works the overnight shift at Stop & Shop on the weekends. Apparently, the night of said murder, Mr. Billy here went to take his break and had his little girlfriend meet him in the back lot. He was giving it to her from the back when he says he heard shots and looked up." Charles and Mox locked eyes. "Billy says he can identify the shooter."

"Fuck!" Mox almost knocked the folder out of Charles' hand.

Charles took a step closer to Mox. "Mr. Daniels, we both know what needs to happen here if you want to continue to operate on these streets. The gun charge is the least of your worries. Ballistics came back and it wasn't the gun that Deandre got killed with." Charles put his hand on Mox's shoulder. "Most you'll do on that is five. I'll see to that, but it's on you to handle this other thing." He grabbed Mox's arm, shook his hand and turned to leave. "Oh, there's a car at the end of the lot waiting to take you to see Priscilla."

Mox stood in the middle of the parking lot looking into the sky at a school of birds dancing through the desiccated, wintry air. He wished he could be a bird and fly away from all the trouble that was bringing him down. He wanted to know where those birds had come from and where they were heading.

He breathed...

SIX

The night Mox was bailed out of the county jail, he went directly to Priscilla's apartment and it would be one of the last nights they would get to spend together for a long time. When he walked into the apartment all the lights were dimmed or completely turned off, but the soft, angelic voice of Whitney Houston could be heard from a distance. She was singing about good love.

He entered the bedroom where Priscilla was stretched out across her queen sized bed wearing a pink, sheer, camisole top with matching crotchless panties. She was mouthing the words to the song with Whitney.

Now you're here like you've been before

And you know just what I need...

It took some time for me to see...

Mox stripped to his boxer shorts and got in the bed beside her. The sweet, inviting, redolent of her Estee Lauder White Linen perfume, inflamed his appetite for sex. The few days he spent away had felt like a lifetime and he desired the gentle, sensuous touch of a female.

"Did you know this was my favorite song?" Priscilla spoke softly and caressed his chest. She ran her hand down his chiseled six-pack and into his boxers.

Mox closed his eyes and let Whitney's harmonic vocals tranquilize him. He was in a calm paradise enjoying how Priscilla slowly stroked his rod until it stiffened in her hand.

Mox lifted his head and looked at Priscilla. "My mother told me that the music you fall in love with is sometimes a reflection of your inner most feelings."

Priscilla mounted Mox and kissed his lips lightly. "Well your mother was right." she continued to cover his face with kisses, making her way to sucking on his earlobe.

He wrapped his arms around her waist and pulled her warm body closer to his so he could feel her vagina pulsating on his hardened muscle. Priscilla kissed down his neck and onto his stomach leaving small rivers of saliva running down his abdomen. When she went to slide his boxers off, she said. “I wanna taste you.” Mox sat up, moved down to the foot end of the bed and Priscilla got on her knees between his legs. She tugged at his dick with both hands and then she licked around the head. Mox grabbed the back of her neck and shoved himself deep inside her warm mouth.

“Ohhh...” he moaned as he watched her pretty lips slide up and down his tool. She coated his ten inch pole with loads of wetness and made a loud slurping sound while doing so .

Mox plucked at her beautiful, protruding, brown nipples with one hand and kept the other on her neck guiding her mouth while he passionately fucked her face. They stood and he lifted her 140 pound frame and buried his face in her nectarous, drippy, vagina.

“Oh, my GOD!! Baby I’m cummin!!!” She tightened her thigh muscles around his neck and choked his face as she convulsed from multiple orgasms.

Mox laid her on her back and positioned himself on top of her. He flicked her nipples with his tongue and slipped his little man inside her steamy wonderland. The fit was perfect. Priscilla reached up and grabbed Mox around his neck and pulled him in close. “I want you to do it slow...”

she put her tongue in his mouth so she could taste herself. “Make love to me, Mox.” her voice was heavenly and appealing. He carefully nudged his long, dark, third leg deeper and deeper into her swollen kitten while Priscilla clawed at his back and tensed up. It felt like he was in her stomach. Mox grabbed her face with both his hands and sucked her soft, sweet lips as he continued his slow, long stroke.

Priscilla felt his cadence increase and he dug further into her canal. “Don’t pull it out.” she whispered in his ear.

On cue, Mox’s body shivered. He sucked her lip harder and gripped the back of her head. “Priscilla... I’m ‘bout to cum.” He mumbled.

“Cum inside me baby.” She climaxed at the same time he did, and they both let out a sigh of ecstasy. They fell asleep engulfed in each other’s arms and he was still inside of her.

Three weeks later, 17 year old Billy Worsham’s body was found on the Northbound side of the Sprain Brook Parkway between Scarsdale and Hastings. He died from multiple gunshots to the chest from a high caliber weapon.

He was the only witness in the Deandre Foster case and now he was gone.

The Westchester County D.A knew they could no longer charge Mox with murder, so he plead out to a firearm possession and was promised 6 years at sentencing, which would be in April.

Mox felt the pressure of being caged as his sentencing day grew closer. He definitely wasn't looking forward to being locked away and he had even thought about running.

Priscilla's hands were shaking as she held the steering wheel and pulled into the county courthouse parking lot. She wanted to stop the car and wail like a two year old baby, but she had to be strong for Mox. She had to prove to him that she could keep the foundation secure and step up as his woman. It was already embedded in her mind that she would continue to stand by his side during the entire sentence; whether it was 6 days or 6 years.

"What are you thinkin' about?" She asked, taking the key out the ignition.

Mox sat up in his seat and put his hand on Priscilla's thigh. "You." he answered.

"What about me?" She placed her hand on top of his.

Mox leaned over and kissed her delicate lips. "I love you." he whispered.

A single droplet fell from the well of her eye and Mox wiped it. He touched her forehead with his lips and told her, "I'll be right back. I gotta take a piss."

"Mox... in the parking lot? What if the police see you?"

"What they gon' do, take me to jail??"

Priscilla couldn't do anything but smile because Mox's sense of humor was one of the main reasons she loved him so much.

She sat in the car and waited for him to come back.

And waited.

And waited some more.

Priscilla sat in the car for seven hours staring at the corner, hoping Mox would step out the shadows at any given moment, but he never did. That day would be the last time she saw Mox Daniels for a long time.

He managed to evade the law for a whole year without incident. They finally caught up to him in Randolph County West Virginia, living in a trailer, tucked off deep in the woods. He was extradited to New York and sentenced in Westchester County court to six years; all to be served in a state correctional facility.

Upstate Correctional Facility

Franklin, NY

(THE SHU)

After serving 3½ years in Clinton Correctional Facility, Mox was moved to Upstate Box because of a tier 3 disciplinary ticket he received for contraband. His cell had been the target of a shakedown and the C.O.s found a homemade shank taped to the bottom of his toilet. Usually he would have been charged with a third degree felony, but the hearing- judge was lenient and all he did was take away Mox's good time and give him a year and a half in the box.

The day Mox was transferred from the county jail to the state prison was one he would remember for the rest of his life. He knew from the time he stepped foot off the bus that he was in a different world.

State and county were two variant monsters that could never be compared. Mox knew that in order for him to survive, he would have to play his hand in a different fashion. The rules weren't the same and the players weren't either, so he was compelled to modify his strategy and adjust his game plan.

2010

The SHU (Special Housing Unit) Aka "The Box" is where the state housed it's most vile inmates. If you were sentenced to time in the box, it was because of a fight or some sort of contraband.

Mox had been in "The Box" for over 500 days, confined to a 9 ½ by 12 ft. double-bunk cell for 23 hours a day. The beds were two steel ledges bolted into the wall and behind them, a steel door which leads to the recreational yard that was about the same size as the cell. It also had a small writing table, some storage space and a shower on the left side. Everything was controlled by the staff from the outside.

During his whole time in Upstate, Mox never had a cellmate that he got along with. They were too loud, too dirty or too tough and not one of one of them lasted more than two weeks. It didn't matter how big or how small they were, none of them could fuck with Mox.

With nothing but time, he sharpened his hand skills along with his mind by shadow boxing and practicing meditation. His whole day was scheduled to a tee. He slept for 6 hours, read for 12, meditated for 5 and went to recreation for 1.

It wasn't until his last ninety days, that Mox was finally placed in a cell with someone decent.

It was 49 year old Priest from Yonkers, New York. He was serving a 13 year sentence for a jewel heist he pulled in 1998 and he only had a year left. The papers say he got away with 3 million in diamonds. The police only recovered diamonds totaling 1.5 million.

Priest was 6'3, 290 pounds, dark skinned and in superior physical shape for a man his age.

Mox took a liking to Priest as soon as he stepped through the gate. It was the aura. His cell was clean. Everything was in order, nothing was out of place and it didn't reek of dirty socks and underarms.

They built a connection, and for the first time Mox could honestly say he found a friend in Priest. All day they would talk. It got to a point where Mox was no longer afraid to share the repressed thoughts of his past. He got a chance to express himself and he wasn't worried about being judged.

One ironic thing they had in common was both of their fathers were taken from them at an early age. It was something they could talk about for hours at a time.

The days passed with ease, and the time came for Mox to make his return back into the world. It was a bittersweet feeling leaving someone that you had just gotten to know, someone you admired, but Mox had a whole life ahead of him and he still had unfinished business to take care of.

He thought about all that was going on in the world and the blessing of a second chance he had been given. He reminisced on the promise he made Casey in a letter he scribed two years ago.

I promise I'll be there when you get drafted to the NBA. He wrote.

And he was going to be able to keep that promise.

"Daniels on the discharge!" The C.O yelled.

Mox shook Priest's hand and gave him a brotherly hug. "I'ma see you when you touch the streets. Be safe in here."

Priest held his hand firm. "Mox, can I ask you a question before you go?"

"Of course old man." Mox shot a playful left jab at Priest's abs.

"Seriously," He looked directly at him. "If you find him, what you gon' do to him?"

Mox stared and for the first time he noticed the color of Priest's eyes. He was drawn to them because they were almost identical to his, maybe a shade or two lighter. He grinned, knowing what Priest was talking about, but he wasn't expecting a question like that. He thought about it for a second.

"First, I'ma ask him why? And then..." the fire in Mox's eyes flickered. "I'ma kill him."

While Mox was locked away, Cleo was playing football and was considered one of the best defensive linemen in the country his senior year. Colleges across the US were scouting the Daniels boy and success looked like a foreseeable destination. A few months before his senior year at high school came to an end, Cleo was awarded a full ride scholarship to play football at Syracuse University. He committed and went on to gain national exposure.

His sophomore year was outstanding. He led the ACC in tackles and sacks which caught the eye of an NFL scout for the New York Jets. Cleo was destined to become a professional superstar, but his uncompassionate outlook on life hindered his decision making and he chose to indulge within the wrong circle of associates.

Ninety days before the 2006 NFL draft, Cleo got shot in the back of his head at a birthday party he attended on the lower East Side of Manhattan. He was seconds away from a flat white line and a pair of pearly gates. He was knocking on the door, but it wasn't his time to arrive.

Cleo was admitted into the Westchester County Medical Center where he slept in a coma for five and a half months. His lifelong dream of becoming an NFL superstar had faded like smoke clouds in a gusty wind.

After a full year of recovery, Cleo's speech, sight and limbs were almost back to normal. Although he had to learn how to talk and walk all over again, his determination fueled his work ethic and he redeemed himself, getting back to his feet as if nothing ever happened.

Cleo came to the realization that his football career was no longer a possibility. It took a minute, but he finally accepted it.

He trained his body daily, going to the gym four days a week. At the time of the shooting, he was an agile 275 pounds and then after surgery he lost 60 pounds, but gained that back plus more during his rehab. He was naturally a big kid, not to mention, he was light on his feet.

Once he gained his confidence back, Cleo started bouncing at nightclubs, mainly in the Bronx and Manhattan area. He built his rep throughout the club scene as the nigga you did not want to bump heads with.

To be so big, Cleo's knuckle game is sharp as a thorn's needle. His temperament is reckless and his attitude is reluctant. To add to that, he's disrespectful when it comes to women. In his warped mind, he believes that they enjoy it and the foul part is he treats his mother no differently.

Cleo's notoriety grew quickly and he built connections with some big names in the drug game as well as the entertainment industry. He was still unsettled about not being able to play professional ball, but the underground way of life seemed to satisfy his cravings.

It was May 2010 and Mox had only been home a month, yet he was already living a lucrative lifestyle. He aligned his old crew from the car wash and went back in business. Quickly he realized things weren't the same as they had been 5 years ago. He no longer had the connect he once cherished, and a piece of his heart was still missing.

Mox had grown up in prison. He became bold and completely certain of himself. The air he exuded was of a boss and those qualities were the ones Cleo recognized while they were growing up. He was afraid of them.

Mox was back in control of his own situation, in command of his own destiny and governing the fate of others. He was beginning to take full advantage of the distinctive qualities God had given him and those countless hours he spentalone gave him the time to reflect on how everyone around him had an impact on his life. He was sometimes even curious about the motives of his own cousin. The resentment was clear cut in Cleo's actions, speech, and disposition, but as they grew older he learned to disguise it and shadow a lot of his true feelings. Mox hadn't considered Cleo to be at threat, and so he brushed it off as a small thing and remained loyal to his family.

One of the reconnections Cleo made was with his old high school teammate, Mikey T at a night club he was working. After they talked for most of the night, Cleo found out about Mikey's family, the Telesco's. He knew who they were and what they did. Recently, he had done some work for Mikey's younger brother, Vito, but at the time he didn't make the connection.

The Telesco's ecstasy ring brought in millions a year. Their only problem was that the labs they had set up were in low income housing areas because they didn't want them in their own communities. It's called product placement, but in doing this, it left them open to stick-ups, murders and problems with the local dealers in those areas.

Mikey T asked Cleo if he could align a protection crew for a new lab they were setting up in the Bronx and that's how the business venture was born.

After seeing that Cleo's crew was official, Mikey brought him to meet his father, Vinny Telesco—aka—The Old Man.

Vinny took a liking to Cleo immediately. He'd been hearing nothing but great stories of his truth and loyalty, so much that he negotiated a percentage of the gross amount from every lab to Cleo as long as he could assemble a protection crew and put an end to all the robberies and violence around the locations.

That's exactly what Cleo did, but in order for it to be done right he needed cousin Mox to run the business and although he was opposed to once again riding in his shadows, there was clearly no other choice in the matter if he wanted it to become profitable, so he sucked it up and dealt with the circumstances the best way he could.

And together they formed **"The Union"**

Structured identical to the American Labor Union, Mox arranged an organization of four Union rep members, not including him and Cleo. The common goal is to band together and create better working conditions for employees.

Negotiations such as wages, rules, complaint procedures, hiring, firing, benefits and workplace safety are discussed through labor contracts. If a worker has a problem or a concern, he/she is to inform the elected Union rep of that borough.

From there, a meeting would be set up and the Union rep would present the information to Cleo and Mox, whereas they would come to a mutual agreement.

Each lab employs eight workers, five in, three out. Two chemists to mix and administer the actual drugs to create the ecstasy, one engineer controlling the compressor machine which produces up to 500 pills every three minutes and two assembly line workers, usually females, to bag up the bundles which consist of 1000 pills per bag. The other three employees are armed guards patrolling the outside areas of the lab.

The rules are strict and enforced in the common area around lab sites. The Union rep's job was to make sure everything ran according to plan. If not, they would have to face Cleo and Mox, and the outcome of that was never a good one.

~THE UNION~

Javier Ramirez, 24 years old, 5ft 9inches, born in Guatemala is the elected Brooklyn Union Rep. He was the one that got Mox the job at Shiny Gleam in 2000. They developed a firm relationship after Havier helped him with the Deandre issue.

Following Mox's incarceration, Javier built his reputation on the streets as a stick-up kid in Yonkers. In 2006, he got pulled over on the New Jersey turnpike with 20 pounds of marijuana and went to the feds for 36 months.

Besides his Union Rep seat, Javier is one of Mox's most trusted men. He handles the supply of most the lower level Brooklyn dealers and alongside that, he owns car lot where he sells used cars.

Frank Williams, 26 years old, 6ft tall, 205 pounds, from Greenburg is the Staten Island Union Rep. Frank earned his nickname, "The Chess Player" because of his strategic maneuvers to elude authorities and outthink his enemies. Back when they worked at the car wash, Frank was on windows and tires, now he's rich, intelligent and handsome with a strong hold on the coke game in Staten Island. Frank was said to be worth millions.

In 2009 he opened up a nightclub in Manhattan called "RED" and hired Cleo as head of security. He also helped

Mox get back in position when he came home by fronting him the buy money on 5 kilo's.

Mox admired the fashion in which Frank did business. He was always truthful and never afraid to speak his mind. On top of that, he controlled a small army of killers who left no witnesses. Frank is another amongst the few who gained Mox and Cleo's trust.

Nate Barnes, 25 years old, 5ft 6inches, 200 pounds, is the Union Rep for the borough of Manhattan. He is by far the most callous of the bunch and is known for his dark glasses, brash attitude and thirst for blood. A short time after leaving Shiny Gleam, Nate became a hired gun for a Peruvian drug cartel and now he has strong ties to some of the world's wealthiest people and is feared globally.

Nate was the only person Mox kept in contact with during his vacation, because he dwelled in the circle of assassins. If anybody could find out information on the man who killed Mox's parents, it was him, so he kept him close.

Papi, 28 years old, 5ft 8inches, 175 pounds, is in control of the Bronx borough. While working with Mox at the car wash, Papi stashed as much money as he could before leaving and was able to open up two bodegas on the

Northside of the BX. Mox mainly used the stores as stash spots.

Just like in prison, if it was a weapon you needed, all you had to do was go see the Spanish dudes. On the streets it was no different. Papi had the illest gun connect heard of and anything The Union needed, he supplied. To be the humblest out the crew, Papi had the means to cause the most damage.

The Union would meet with the Italians on the first Sunday of the New Year at the Pallazzo Hotel in Las Vegas to discuss the previous month's earnings and go over the outline for the current quarter. Any disputes Union Reps have toward each other are addressed at the meet and usually taken care of.

The meeting was less than two weeks away and Cleo was hoping that everything would go well. He was aware of the tension between his cousin, Mox, and the Italians, but he was pretty sure it could be diffused before things get out of hand. What Cleo didn't know was that Mox had his own agenda and he was playing by his own set of rules.

SEVEN

A dense fog settled on the quiet night as Cleo stood, gun in hand, red beam dancing on Supreme's forehead. He honestly didn't know how it had gotten to this point, but what he did know was that shit was about to get real.

His heart beat at a high rate and his stomach was in a twist, but he had to get this done. It was his only chance to prove himself to Mox.

His hands, covered in black leather gloves, he held the .40 caliber weapon firmly. His breathing was heavy after running half a block; Cleo wasn't a little dude. He stood 6 ft. 3 inches and weighed in at 302 pounds, so that half a block chase had him wheezing.

"You had to make me run, huh?" Cleo gasped. "It didn't have to come to this." he looked directly into Supreme's his eyes.

Not a speckle of fear was visible. Preme wasn’t a sucker; he was a certified gangster. "You ain’t built for no bodies, Cleo." He drawled. "You a business man, you ain’t no killa."

Cleo thought for a second, maybe he was right. Then again, maybe he wasn't.

"You know what?" He took a step closer. “You absolutely right, Supreme." Cleo placed the cold steel barrel to the middle of his eyebrows. "This is business, never personal."

He squeezed the trigger with his index finger and a round was released through the chamber. It created a deafening sound that could be heard for blocks.

The slug blew half of Supreme's brain onto the brick wall and his body collapsed to the moist pavement.

Cleo stood still for what felt like minutes, but were actually seconds, staring at Supreme's empty body. Not even realizing how far he had gone. He snapped out of his trance and departed the scene before police arrived.

Mox gripped the steering wheel of the all black Denali as it muscled down the highway in route to his destination. He sang along with Sade's soft, soulful voice as *Soldier of Love* whispered through the speakers.

I'm a solider of love...

Today Mox wasn't feeling good at all and that usually wasn't the case, but because of a sudden tragedy, there was a major shift in the plans.

The music went silent and a beeping sound came through the speakers. It was Mox's bluetooth connection. He looked at the display on his cell phone and quickly hit accept. He hoped it was the call he had been waiting on.

"Wassup?" He answered.

"That little birdie that's been singin' outside your window is no longer a problem." The caller assured.

"Beautiful. That's why I love you." Mox smiled and reached his hand over to caress the leg of the beautiful, young lady sitting in the passenger seat. "Meet me at Vito's spot, tomorrow afternoon. Peace."

Tamika quickly pushed Mox's hand off her leg and sucked her teeth. "Who da fuck was that?"

“What I tell you about minding my business, Tamika... jus shut the fuck up and enjoy the ride. Please."

Tamika's neck twisted and she wore a look of astonishment. "Nigga, I don't know who da fuck you think you talkin' to, but I damn sure ain't one of dem bird bitches you use to fuckin' wit."

Mox smirked and hit the right blinker indicating that he would be getting off at the next exit. He really didn't like Tamika, personality wise, but she was gorgeous and she had a name and that’s all that mattered to Mox at this time. He wasn't a fool; he knew she was only with him because he was a young, street nigga with a lot of money, but he also had his own personal reasons for befriending her.

"What make you so different, Tamika?" He questioned. "Sit here and tell me you ridin' in my shit cause you like me. Go head and tell me that lie. You fuckin' me because I got money, Tamika; I'm that nigga!" He shouted, pulling up to a red light.

Tamika rolled her eyes knowing he was absolutely correct, but she didn't give a fuck. This was her game. She only dealt with dudes that had money and she sure wasn't concerned whether it was legal or illegal. Her mentality was, use what you got, to get what you want.

Once they exited the highway all the roads were pitch black. Mox came to a stop and looked right to left for a street sign to help him figure out where he was. He and Tamika had been on the road six and a half hours in route to Danville, Virginia from New York City.

Once he recognized the area, he relaxed. The light turned green and Mox pulled over to the curb.

"What you pullin' over for, Mox?"

Mox put the truck in park, hit the overhead light, reached to the backseat and grabbed a newspaper article. He glanced at it, shook his head and held it up for Tamika to see.

"You see this?" Mox said.

The clipping had a picture of a brown skinned kid with wavy hair and a chipped tooth smile. He was standing in the middle of a basketball court holding a ball.

The headline read: ***'First round NBA draft pick killed in robbery'***

Tamika looked confused. "I don't understand?"

Mox leaned his seat back and snatched the pearl handled nine from his waistline. He looked at Tamika and calmly placed it on the middle console. “I’ma give you another chance. Please don’t lie to me. I’m beggin’ you.”

Tamika's nerves raged; she was terrified. *I should’ve listened.*

They told her this nigga was crazy.

She could barely get the words out. "Ye...yes, I remember."

"Good." Mox smiled. "Now, take a real good look at this kid’s face." he said, pointing at the young man’s face.

Tamika took the clipping and put it to her face to see it clearer. She knew who it was, but now he looked even more familiar.

She glanced at Mox.

He sat, smiling. The same smile the kid had minus the chipped tooth. She couldn't believe it.

"You can't believe it right?" Mox was holding the pearl handled weapon in his right hand, pointed directly at Tamika's head. "That was my little brother, Tamika." Mox cried.

She reached for the door handle, but the door was locked.

She tried the unlock button, but nothing happened, so she screamed to the top of her lungs. "HELP! PLEASE! SOMEBODY HELP ME!!"

Mox switched the gun to his left hand and wiped the tears from his cheek. "Bitch, you can scream for help all you want. Ain't nobody gon' hear you."

He wasn't lying either. The Denali he was driving was a one of one, exclusive, presidential edition. Fit with bombproof exterior, soundproof interior and right now, parked on the side of the road, in the middle of nowhere; the black matte color made it invisible.

Tamika continued screaming and trying to escape the armed fortress. A swift blow to the side of her face with the butt of the gun calmed her down.

She curled over, holding her wound, head between her legs.

"I loved my brother, Tamika." Mox sniffled. "He was my heart."

Casey Daniels was considered the best shooting guard to come out of New York in the last 5 years. He led UCONN to a National Championships and also led the Big East in scoring.

Casey was one of kind and he had just signed a twenty million dollar endorsement deal with Nike. He earned the top pick in the draft and was headed to Washington to play with the Wizards, but his life was cut short when Tamika and an accomplice robbed and shot him in his hotel room. They took $7,500 in cash, a Hublot wristwatch worth five thousand and his life, which was priceless.

When he received the phone call from Cleo about the murder, Mox wanted to believe it was a joke, but then he realized nobody around him joked about things of that nature. The news was sudden and overwhelming. A horrified feeling of emptiness and discomfort quickly settled in the pit of his stomach, his other half was gone and he had already been living with the tragic double homicide of both parents, now this. At the time he was given the news, he was on his way to celebrate Casey's remarkable accomplishments, but sadly, that intended celebration would be halted forever.

The only information Mox had on the incident was what Cleo told him about a female named Tamika, who supposedly was the last person seen with Casey in the hotel, that and a bunch of mixed up stories from the police and media about an accomplice.

A week or so after the tragedy, Mox had Tamika's full name, address, date of birth, cell-phone number, house number, social security number, credit score and anything else he needed to get in contact with her. He followed her and monitored her movements for days until he had her routine figured out and then he approached her. He knew she wouldn't know who he was because not many people did. He did his best to keep his lifestyle away from his brother's success.

Mox was familiar with the type of female Tamika was, he attracted her kind all the time. It only made it easier for him to turn their social acquaintance into a night of heavy breathing, shit talking and ass slapping. After he fucked her a few times, he led her to believe she was going to assist him in moving some work out of state. Of course her greed, thirst and perilousness went uncontested. There wasn't a doubt in her mind that Mox could possibly be her next victim, but she was clueless as to what was really going on. It didn't take much and when she went for the bait, she got hooked.

Mox was furious. He tried to gathering himself, he cocked the barrel of the handgun and a bullet slid into the chamber.

His eyes, filled with fury.

A rainfall of tears ran down Tamika's pretty face smudging the make-up she had on. "Please, Mox, don't do this. I'm... I'm sorry."

"My brother had a bright future, Tamika. He was the only one that graduated high school, he was making something of his self and he was my ticket outta this lifestyle... you got him got killed.... you fuckin' bitch!"

Tamika looked into Mox's eyes and knew she didn't stand a chance. There was no escaping her fate.

Bizarre and distorted visions of Casey and his parents flashed before Mox's eyes. The gruesome scene in which his mother and father were murdered was right in front of him. He was standing in that exact room, his little brother hanging over his shoulder, looking down at their parent's, mutilated bodies.

Mox wiped his face of tears a second time and watched Tamika as she rocked back and forth in the cushy, leather seat; praying. He pressed the gun to her head. “Who set this shit up? Who was you wit!?”

She never stopped rocking and then mumbled, “I don’t know.”

“Bitch!” He pressed harder against her temple with the weapon. “Stop lying to me!”

“I swear I’m not lying.” Through cries she tried to explain. “All they told me was the time they would be there and how much they were going to pay me. When he came in...” her breathing was erratic. “I was in the bathroom.” she continued to rock. “Please God, don’t let him kill me. I’m sorry. I swear. I’m sorry...”

"You can get down on your knees and pray to the heavens above and ask God for whatever it is you want, but until you believe in those words, the only thing you doing is wasting your breath."

The barrel jumped back and the slug pushed Tamika's head to the passenger seat window. Her brains decorated the glass.

Mox reached over, snatched the ten thousand dollar Tiffany necklace off her neck, pushed her body from the truck and left her on the side of road in the middle of Virginia.

EIGHT

Vito's Bar & Grill - White Plains, New York

The doorbells jingled as Cleo entered the dimly lit restaurant. Delicate sounds of Frank Sinatra whispered at a low tone and the tasteful aroma of sausage and peppers soaked the air. Cleo always smiled when he stepped into Vito's because he knew he would get a good meal.

He waved and greeted the aged white guy behind the long, oak wood bar. "Tony, what's goin' on?"

"Nothin' much, Cleo. Good to see ya." He replied.

"Same here."

Cleo continued to the back, acknowledging the few patrons scattered throughout the restaurant eating and drinking. He spotted Vito sitting in a booth at the rear with two females. "Excuse me, ladies. Vito my man, what's good?"

Vito excused himself from the table, shook Cleo's hand and they walked over to a different booth.

"Mox went too far this time, Cleo." He took a seat. "I might not be able to save you guys on this one." Vito hissed.

"Save us, from what?"

"C'mon, Cleo yous know how the rules go. Supreme was like a made guy. I mean, he ain't family or nuttin' like that, but yous can't just go whackin' off any and everyone yous please. It's structure here."

Cleo laughed and sipped his water. "Structure, huh?" He stared with unconcern at the man sitting across the table from him. "You wanna know what I think, Vito? I think you're full of shit, but hey," he shrugged his shoulders. "that's just my opinion, right?"

Vito's blood seethed and his body language revealed his distaste. *The nerve of this nigger, walking in here, talking to me like that,* he thought. "Cleo, your filthy mouth is gonna get you inna a lot of trouble, I tell ya."

Cleo smiled. "We'll cross that bridge when we come to it."

Cleo meant that too. He didn't fear the Italians at all. He was willing to go head up with anyone in the way, and the Telesco crime family was not exempt.

Vito Telesco was third in rank, which would make him Capo under the hierarchy. His older brother, Mikey T is Underboss and their father, Vinny is the Boss.

Vito's Bar & Grill was also a front for an underground casino that operated from midnight till 5am. The walls were made of brick, the ceilings, a dark tin and Christmas trimmings hung all year 'round. Rather than booking reservations, Vito designated tables to regular customers once a week. Privileges were allotted depending not on monetary heft or G status but, for the most part, on loyalty. Nowhere else could a person own a table like a condominium.

Only a select few are admitted and those few are well known and respected. Most of them came to Vito's to conduct business that couldn't be handled in an office.

"So, where's your boy at?" Vito asked. "It's fuckin' 3:30 and he still ain't here."
Cleo ignored Vito's question for the moment. He summoned the waiter and ordered a double shot of Remy Martin.

"Be easy, he's on his way."

Vito mumbled something under his breath, but Cleo didn't catch it.

"You said something, Vito?? He questioned.

As soon as Vito went to speak, Mikey T walked through the door.

"My colored brother, Cleo! What the fuck is goin' on guy?" He yelled.

Unlike Vito, Mikey T and Cleo were the best of friends. They attended high school together and both were starting defensive linemen on the varsity football team.

Mikey T knew his position in the family; he just didn't have the same views as they did regarding blacks. He possessed a genuine love for Cleo that was real, but he would never go against his blood.

Cleo pushed his seat back and stood to greet Mikey. "My Caucasian twin, Mikey mutha-fuckin T!" he embraced him.

"It's been a minute, eh, Cleo. Good to see you, bro. You still big as a house I see."

They laughed together.

"That's good eatin' Mikey. How's The Old Man?"

"Hangin' in there. You know how it is. Lately he's back n forth to the doc. This freakin' diabetes is killin' him, and you know how The Old Man is... he don't listen to nobody."

While Mikey and Cleo got reacquainted, Vito boiled. Mikey hadn't even acknowledged his own brother and here he was laughing and joking.

"How's my little bro doin'?" He finally asked, tapping Vito's chest.

Vito got up from his chair to hug his older brother. He wanted to tell him how he really felt, but circumstances of that nature could never be discussed in public. Besides, Mikey knew Vito disliked that he showed Cleo so much respect, but there was little he could do about it.

"Could be better, could be worse." Vito answered.

Mikey took a seat at the table. "Who ya tellin'. So, Cleo...eh, where's Mox?"

On cue, Mox appeared at the front door, black as night sporting a pearl white, fox bomber with the hat to match.

The five inch, Cuban cigar he puffed produced a thick, white cloud of smoke.

"Speak of the devil and in he walks." Cleo laughed.

"Look at this fuckin' clown." Vito barked.

Mikey jumped up. "Hey, cool it Vito." He approached Mox. "No smokin' in here, bro."

Mox stopped at the table, took another puff of his cigar and blew the smoke into the air.

"Fuck you, Mikey. Tell them white guys over there to stop smokin'. We came to talk business, correct?"

"Correct."

"So, this is my proposal and rest assured my partner feels the same way. Right, Cleo?"

Cleo didn't speak; he just nodded his head. Truth was, he didn't know what the fuck Mox was about to say. They spoke on a few percentages, but Cleo told him it was too early to get those types of numbers. They were just getting in good with the Italians and to demand a higher percentage on all endeavors was something Cleo knew they wouldn't go for.

Mox continued. "We want a piece of Queens."

Vito cut his eyes over to Mikey. They both held a look of surprise. "Queens??" they said, in unison.

"Yeah, Queens." Mox repeated.

"I don't know what you talking about, Mox." Mikey lied.

"You know what I'm talkin' about Mikey... Astoria. That warehouse, seven hundred thousand a month. Any of this ring a bell?"

"You're a funny fuckin' guy, you know that, Mox?" Mikey snarled. "You should be here discussing how much compensation you gonna give The Old Man for knocking off one of his major dealers."

"Fuck, Supreme! That nigga was a snitch! Cleo, what's thirty-five percent of seven hundred thousand? Quick."

"Is this true, Cleo?" Mikey asked.

Cleo rubbed his fingers together. "Yeah, it's true." he paused and looked at Mox. "Two hundred and forty-five thousand."

Mox kept smoking his cigar. "It don't matter anyway, Supreme is dead. I came to talk about Queens and our two hundred and forty-five thousand a month."

"The Old Man still needs something," Mikey bargained.

"Well the Old Man ain't getting shit from me till I get a piece of Queens."

Vito raised up. "Hey, watch your fuckin' mouth, guy."

"Fuck you, Vito!"

Cleo stood. "Mox, chill."

"Nah, Cleo. Fuck these EYE-Talians!" He stressed. "We don't need these muthafuckas... they need us!"

Mikey fixed his tie. "Cleo, talk to your boy. Maybe come back tomorrow. Things might be different, eh?"

"Yeah, tell ‘em to shut up, Cleo before I do it myself." Vito added.

Mox smiled at the two brothers. If he really wanted to, he could kill them both right now, but the chances of him and Cleo surviving were slim to none.

The only reason he hadn't started a war was because the money was coming in at rapid rates. The Italians controlled the ecstasy market throughout the five boroughs as far as the manufacturing went, but Mox and Cleo provided the muscle and protection for those labs to operate.

They produced thousands of ecstasy pills a day that were sold and distributed to wholesalers who, in turn, re-sell them at market rate which varies from $7 to $10 a pill. At the time, the four major manufacturing labs are located in Brooklyn, Staten Island, Manhattan and the Bronx.

Each factory roughly accumulated five to eight hundred thousand dollars a month in revenue and Mox and Cleo's cut was 20% of everything.

The Telesco's thought they were being slick by secretly opening up another lab in Queens thinking Cleo and Mox wouldn't be too worried about it. They were wrong. Mox caught wind of the situation and wanted in. Cleo, on the other hand, really didn't care, but what's right is right. They made an agreement and the Italians were trying to renig.

Mox removed the hat from his head and grilled Vito. "Try it, Vito. I dare you." They eyed each other intensely.

"C'mon, Mox." Cleo tapped his shoulder. "Mikey, we gotta make this thing right. I'll be in contact. And tell the Old Man I said, get well."

Mikey frowned, "Sure, Cleo." Then he remembered. "Oh, I almost forgot; sorry for your loss, Casey was a good kid, it's a fucked up situation."

"Yeah, it is." He replied.

Cleo and Mox stepped out the door and into the windy, pedestrian filled streets. Four days before Christmas and the holiday shoppers were out in abundance, scurrying to get their last minute gifts.

Cleo pulled his cell phone out to call a cab.

"You still fuckin' wit' them cabs, huh?" Mox questioned, knowing exactly what Cleo was doing. He couldn't understand why he hadn't bought a car yet. He had more than enough money.

“I can't find a truck comfortable enough for my big ass," he joked.

He wasn't lying though, Cleo shopped around for a new truck, but the ones he test-drove didn't fit him the way he wanted. He wasn't in a rush to buy a vehicle any way; he took cabs everywhere he went.

"Man, fuck that cab. I got the truck around the corner."

“Cool, but Mox you gotta be easy with these Italians. Right now ain’t the time to be stirring up a war.”

“Fuck them degos, Cleo!” He fumed. “Pasta eatin’ muthafuckas. I don’t trust ‘em and you shouldn’t either. Those assholes knew exactly what they were doing when they opened up that lab in Queens. They thought we wouldn’t find out, but I want mines, and if I gotta get it in blood, so be it.”

Cleo knew Mox was hotheaded, but he wasn’t about to let stupidity come in the way of millions.

He took a deep breath. “We don’t need any more problems, Mox. That’s all I’m sayin’. We gettin’ good money from these dudes and The Old Man’s beginning to show some leniency. Let’s not fuck up a great a situation.”

“It may be great for you, but it ain’t great for me. I want more.” Mox said, starting the truck.

Gluttony was something that Cleo despised. The way he saw it was, the only thing greed could get you is a pine box or a hundred years in a cell. He didn't want either of the two.While in the truck, something dawned on Cleo. "Mox, what about the bitch?" he asked.

Mox pulled the truck from the curb. "I left that bitch on the side of the Roanoke River." he laughed loudly.

NINE

Pellegrino's Restaurant, Little Italy, NYC

December 22nd 2010

Pellegrino's Restaurant, located on the infamous Mulberry Street in Little Italy is a fairly new establishment mixed in with hundreds of years of Italian heritage.

Tucked away in the cut, Pellegrino's serves as one of the Telesco's favorite hangouts. Frequently, you can catch Mikey or Vito sitting at a table feasting on a plate of penne al la vodka and salad. At times you may even catch Vinny Telesco himself sitting at the bar.

Sunny tossed his cigarette to the ground and stomped on it before he walked through the doors to Pellegrino's. The restaurant was packed.

Upon entering, he removed his hat and unbuttoned his wool pea coat. He slid past the two couples waiting to be seated and walked over to the bar area.

"Lemme get a straight gin. No rocks." He told the bartender.

Sunny looked around for a familiar face. Seeing none, he tossed his drink back and ordered another one. It was like a flame burning in his chest. He was warming up now. His nerves were calming and he was feeling more like himself. He felt normal. The confidence he previously lacked was building up like a snowball racing down the Appalachian Mountains.

His fears evaporated like boiling water in a pot.

He was ready.

He turned to exit the restaurant and stopped short as if he had forgotten something.

"Hey!" He screamed, turning back, reaching into his pants. The shotgun being lifted from his waist was sawed off. "Mox says, suck his dick!"

The explosion that followed was ear-splitting. Standing patrons fell to the floor, waitresses panicked in fear for their lives.

Sunny put two more slugs into the half of gun, cocked it and pulled the trigger once more.

The smoke clouds were so thick, Sunny could barely see in front of him. The bartender, crouched behind the marble bar, nervously fingered his old .38 snub-nosed. He was waiting for a clear view. Quickly he stood up and let off four shots, two striking Sunny in the chest.

The impact slammed Sunny's frail frame to the floor. He tried to crawl to the front door, but he wasn't able to. Just trying to breathe was difficult enough. He gagged on his own blood. Once his body shook and his heart stopped beating. It was over.

The few customers and employees who didn't get hit, scurried to the exit and pushed their way out of the restaurant and into the streets.

In the rear of the restaurant, ten feet away from the kitchen, Vito poked his head up slightly above the table that hid him. He was terrified, but he couldn't show it.

He lifted himself up and tried brushing some tomato sauce off his suit. "Shit!" he cursed, checking his body for any wounds. Trembling, Vito, pulled his phone from his pocket and dialed a number.

Someone picked up on the other end. "Vito?"

"Mikey, we got a problem." He whispered.

"Lick the head... yeaahh... ohhhhh I love that shit." Mox moaned. He bit his bottom lip and let his head fall back on the plush leather.

Kim held his dick with two hands and slid her tongue up and down his long, heavy shaft. A long stream of saliva hung from her chin as she devoured his thick, chocolate Mr. Goodbar. Kim loved sucking Mox's dick. It was huge. Each time she tried to deep throat, she gagged and tears came out of her eyes.

Mox raised his head and palmed Kim's soft ass with both his hands. He slapped her cheek that had a tattoo of black panther on it.

"Ooooohhh! Wait...open your mouth. Ahhhhhhhh!??."

Kim sucked until Mox shot a load of warm, pearl white cum all over her face.

She licked her fingers, blew a kiss at the camera and smiled.

"Mox, you always taste good."

He picked his cigar up out the ashtray, lit it and then hit stop on his HD camera.

"You should be a movie star, Kim." He picked his pants up off the floor. "I swear to God you put on an Oscar winning performance every-mutha-fuckin-time." He laughed.

"I need a favor, Mox." Kim asked.

"A favor?"

"Yeah. Can I hold some money?" She asked, snapping her bra straps.

"Hold some money?" Mox repeated, sarcastically. But he actually didn't have a problem giving Kim money. Only because he knew she was an independent female who took care of her responsibilities and this was the first time she had ever asked him for anything other than some dick.

Mox chuckled.

"I'm serious, Mox, it's been rough for me raising little man by myself. Shit, every penny I get goes toward bills and the baby. I just wanna treat myself to somethin' nice."

"Where that little nigga's father at?"

"Who the fuck knows, Mox. I aint spoke to that nigga since the day I told him I was pregnant." Kim barked. She flicked through the channels on the remote. "And my brother ain't helpin' out either; he runnin' around in the streets somewhere. When was the last time you saw Supreme, Mox?"

Hearing his name made Mox's antennas rise. He was trying to be cool. "Supreme, who?" He asked as if he didn't know.

"My brother, Supreme, nigga. Who else?"

"Oh, Preme," Mox slowly repeated. "Shit, I ain't seen dat nigga, Preme in like...two weeks; maybe three." He lied.

Mox had honestly forgotten that Supreme was Kim's older brother, not that it would have stopped anything, but maybe he would have thought on it a little longer. He really admired Kim and not just because she sucked good dick, but because she was a smart and outgoing person. The few females Mox dealt with were money hungry groupies. Kim was different, but her brother was a snitch, so he had to go.

How could he explain to Kim that her only brother was dead, and on top of that, he was the one who orchestrated the hit. Her poor little heart would be crushed and Mox just couldn't live with that.

With concern in her voice, she said, "Well, I hope he's alright."

Mox's cell phone rang and at the same time someone was knocking on Kim's front door. Seeing the caller ID, he grabbed the phone and answered it.

"Gimmie a second and I'ma call you back." He spat quickly, pressing end before Cleo could speak. "Get the door, Kim."

Mox put his sweatshirt on and glanced down at the Smith & Wesson.9 millimeter lying on the end table next to the sofa.

"Who is it?" Kim sang as she pranced down the hallway to the front door. Without looking through the peephole, she undid the locks.

Hulk sneered when the door came open and spoke, "Vito sends his regards." he chuckled, lifting twin .50 caliber desert eagles.

Two shots pushed Kim's 130 pound body five feet down the hallway. She was dead on contact.

When Mox heard the blast, he snatched his gun from the table, reached in his pocket and slipped the clip in. Quickly, he let off six shots hoping it could buy him some time, and then he got low.

"C'mon, muthafuckas!" He whispered under his breath, holding his weapon firmly.

Hulk stepped over Kim's stiff corpse and peeked around the corner. He pushed his back off the wall and let the twin 50's rip. The small missiles tore through the air crashing into anything in the way. Glass shattered, dust and smoke filled the atmosphere and Mox sat composed, awaiting his chance.

He counted under his breath. "4, 3, 2— "Hearing both guns click, Mox knew they were empty. He sprang to his feet gunning like Joe Montana on 4th down with the game on the line.

Every slug that came through the barrel slammed into Hulk's wide chest, dropping him to the plush carpet. He was choking on blood, but he still had a bit of life in him.

Mox waited to see if there were any more shooters and then he made his way over to where Hulk was. Seeing that he was still breathing, he tried to roll the 6'4 240 pound man over on his back and after two attempts, he finally got it.

"Who sent you?" He growled, shoving the hot gun barrel to Hulk's temple.

Surveying the apartment, he could see Kim's petite frame lying in a pool of blood, which only intensified his anger. "I'ma ask you again. Who—"

Hulk tried to speak. "Vi... to," his words were low, but Mox heard him. "Said, fuu--ck you."

Mox stood and emptied the clip into Hulk's stomach.

Vito?

He cut his thinking short and rushed over to Kim. His heart fluttered, and immediately tears washed his face. He dropped to his knees. He couldn't believe it. He picked her up and held her in his hands.

"Kim," He whimpered. "Kim, wake up baby." Mox wiped the stream of blood seeping from her lips just as he had done with his mother years ago. His heart felt like it was about to explode. Hearing sirens in the distance, he jumped out of his daze and carried Kim's limp body to the sofa.

Mox stood still for a moment looking around. *Damn.* He thought. *My prints all over this muthafucka.* It wasn't enough time to wipe the entire apartment down, so Mox threw his boots on, snatched his coat and went to make his exit.

"Oh, shit." He turned on his heels and went back to get his HD camera. "Definitely can't leave this."

Vito paced back and forth in his shiny, hard bottom shoes, tapping the wood floor with each step. "I can't believe this shit." he cursed.

"Vito, sit down!" The Old Man hollered from his chair. His voice, hoarse from bronchitis.

Vinny Telesco had been watching his youngest son have a nervous breakdown for the past forty-five minutes. He had no clue of the situation, but all the bickering and foul language gave him reason to believe something transpired.

"What happened, Vito?" Mikey questioned.

Nervous, Vito pulled a cigarette from his pack and lit it. Normally The Old man would make a big deal of him smoking in the house, but he let him get away with it today.

"Vito, you hear your brother talkin' to you?"

"It was a fuckin' hit, Mikey. That black bastard Mox put a hit on us." He answered.

"Mox?"

"Yeah, Mox."

"When'd this happen, Vito?" The Old Man asked.

Vito took a long drag of his cigarette and blew the smoke out.

"Bout a hour and a half ago." He puffed the cigarette. "I slid down to Pellegrino's to have some lunch, ya know, a lil' penne n whatnot and this fuckin' junky, umm...what's his name?" Vito thought hard. "Oh yeah, Sunny. Sunny Gallano. He walks in and you know me, I'm duckin' the fuckin' guy 'cause he's always beggin'. So, I'm in the back by the kitchen and all of a sudden I see this fuckin' loser he's standing in the middle of the joint holding a fuckin' sawed off." Vito took another drag and continued. "So, you know me, Mikey. I go for my rivoltella (Pistol) and we shoot it out." He fibbed.

Immediately, The Old Man knew Vito was telling a lie about shooting it out. He raised both these boys and knew exactly what they were capable of. Vito was a bit on the timid side. He just used the family name as a crutch.

Mikey found it hard to believe also. "So, you twos is shootin' it out in the restaurant, huh? Then what?" he inquired.

"I finally got a clear look through all the smoke and I hit the guy." Vito lied again.

"So you took him down?" Mikey said. "Where does Mox come in this at?"

"Fuckin' Sunny screams out his name before he starts shootin' up the place."

The Old Man looked at his eldest son. "Mikey, what you think?"

“I don’t know, Pop, sounds kinda funny to me.” Mikey tried to make light of the situation. “I mean, why would Mox get drunk Sunny to do a hit for him? It just doesn’t make sense to me.”

“It makes perfect fuckin’ sense, Mikey. That fuckin’ moulie wants to start a war!” Vito argued.

The Old Man had heard enough. “Cool it, Vito.” he cautioned. “Here’s what we do.” He turned to Mikey. “Vegas is coming up in a few days; see what Cleo has to say about this. Until then, sit tight.”

A dim-witted expression came over Vito’s face. “Too late.”

“What do you mean too late, Vito?” The Old man questioned.

“It’s too late, pop. I sent, Hulk.”
“Ahh, nah, Vito, what you go and do that for?” Mikey steamed.

The Old Man struggled to stand up from his chair. He was furious. It wasn’t that he was afraid of Mox, it was the fact that he has so much respect for Cleo that he didn’t want to harm him, let alone go to war with him.

He slung Vito a look that spoke volumes and then faced his eldest. "Mikey. Get Tommy on the phone. Tell him we got a problem."

TEN

"Chris, make the next right and then a left at the stop sign." Cleo directed, sitting in the back seat of his favorite livery cab.

The town car slowed at the stop sign and Chris hit the left blinker.

"One day I might be able to own one of these nice houses back here." He dreamed.

"Nothing's impossible, Chris. If you work hard enough I'm sure you can get anything you want."

The cab cruised at a moderate 15 miles per hour down Tall Spruce Circle in Kensington Woods. It was one of the wealthiest areas in New Rochelle, New York.

Cleo sat back staring out the window at the placid scenery. He wished his life could be as simple as some of the families in this community, but it wasn't and now it looked like it was going to get worse.

“One twenty one Kensington Circle, sir.”

He pushed the door open and hopped out the Town car.

“Aight, Chris, I’m good.” He said, peeling a crisp hundred dollar bill from his stack.

“You sure you don't want me to wait, Cleo?”

“Nah, go ‘head. If I need you, I’ll call.” Cleo replied.

Cleo hurried down the driveway to Mox’s 3500 square foot estate. Usually, when Cleo got to the front door it was open because Mox would see him on the surveillance cameras. Today it wasn’t, so he rang the doorbell.

“C’mon, Mox open the door.” He whispered. Then he rang it again.

After two more rings he stepped back to get a view of the second floor and yelled. “Yo, Mox!”

A shadow moved behind the blinds and then they slid open.

Mox was standing in his robe, holding his AK47 trying to see who the fuck was yelling his name. Noticing Cleo, he rushed down to open the door.

He barely passed the threshold and Mox was already screaming.

“They killed Kim.” He slammed the door shut. Mox clenched a bottle of Perrier Jouet in his right hand.

“What the fuck are you talkin’ about?” Cleo was confused. He followed Mox into the living room.

“Fuck them spaghetti head muthafuckas!”

“Mox, I told you now wasn't the time to be startin’ a war. We can't afford that right now.”

Mox looked at Cleo like he was crazy. “I ain’t start shit. They kill one of ours, we kill one of theirs. You know how this game is played. Kim didn’t deserve that.”

Cleo was still lost. “Hold up...hold up. I don't know nothing about Kim or none of that shit. What the fuck happened at Pellegrino’s?” he questioned.

"Pelle, who?" Mox laughed, but it wasn't a joke. He took a swig from the bottle then plopped down onto his chaise lounge.

"Pellegrino's, Mox. Don't act like you don't know what I'm talkin' about. You sent that fuckin' drunk in there to shoot up the place."

Mox's brow furred. He stood up and faced Cleo. "I aint sent nobody to do nothing... and I don't know what the fuck a Pelleninos or Pellepinos or..." He hesitated. "Whatever that is. All I know is that I was getting' my dick sucked and the phone rang. I saw it was you, so I picked up. Right after I said I'ma call you back, somebody start knocking on the door." Mox tipped the bottle again. "Kim went to see who it was and all I heard was a cannon. I had to let a couple go in order to buy some time and then I got low."

Cleo interrupted. "Aight, so what that got to do with the Italians?"

"Are you serious, Cleo?" Mox couldn't understand Cleo's reaction. "That big, pasta eatin" muthafucka spit Vito's name out before I fixed him."

"C'mon, Mox stop Lyin!" He yelled.

Mox got offended. “First of all, lower ya muthafuckin’ voice in my crib. Second, when have I ever lied about some shit as serious as this?” His eyes were trained on Cleo. “Don’t let ‘em brainwash you cousin. You of all people know how I get down.” Cleo didn’t know how things would play out. The monthly sit down was days away and here he was stuck in the middle of a potential war with the Telesco Crime Family.

“Aight, listen, let me apologize for yellin’ in your home, but this is what gotta happen.” He took a seat. "We got a few days until Vegas, Mox. I know they killed shorty, but I need you to be cool until we sort this out. I spoke to The Old Man and as long as you don't move, they won’t move.”

Mox shook his head. “I don't trust ‘em.”

“Trust me, Mox. Please?”

Christmas day came and light snow flurries fell from the sky like confetti. Children were out in full swing by 9:30am riding new bikes and racing remote control cars.

Hustlers huddled on street corners hustling and the homeless sought refuge from the blistering cold weather.

Even though Mox had never received a gift on Christmas, it was still one of his favorite holidays. Growing up, he always looked forward to waking up early on this day and rushing across the hall to Cleo's house just to play with his toys. Cleo didn't get much either, but it was more than what Mox had.

He put his Moncler bubble coat on and tied a scarf around his neck. He knew to dress appropriately because he would be standing in the wind for most of the day.

His phone rang as he was getting into his truck.

"Hello?"

"Mox, I think I'ma cool out today. I don't feel like being bothered." Cleo said.

He was anticipating this call. For his first Christmas home, Mox spent a few thousand dollars on gifts for some of the less fortunate kids in the community. He rounded up a few teens from the Boys & Girls Club and they were going to pull up to the projects in a big trailer and hand out gifts to everyone who came out.

“C’mon Cleo, It’s my first Christmas back. Don’t make me come over there and snatch your big ass out the bed. It’s for the kids, man.”

“I aint feeling it Mox. I got a lot of shit on my mind.”

“You aint the only one. Last night I had to make that call to Kim’s people. Imagine how I’m feelin’.”

“Word. I might come through. No guarantees though.”

“Aight. Peace.” Mox tossed the cell phone in the passenger seat. He knew he wasn’t coming. It was the same thing every time with Cleo. If it didn’t benefit him in any way, shape or form, he wasn’t with it. His selfish ways hadn’t changed at all. They just grew worse.

The trailer pulled into the parking lot and the children's faces lit up like Christmas lights when the back doors to the massive vehicle opened up. Mox and his handful of helpers stood, smiling. Red and white Santa hats atop their heads and a plethora of toys surrounding them.

Mox lived for days like this because he was once one of the less fortunate. Each time he gave a gift out and was thanked, his smile spread wider. The hood loved Mox, especially this hood.

From his peripheral, Mox spotted a familiar face. He jumped down from the back of the trailer and advanced toward her.

"Priscilla?" He called.

The joyless young lady stared at Mox, trying to recognize his face. Her hair was in shambles and her garments were unkempt. Drug use was obvious, but she still seemed to have a sparkle of flair lingering.

In less than a minute, she recalled his face. How could she not remember? She grinned, but then her pleasure immediately turned to sorrow.

"You see what these streets did to me, Mox?"

"You stronger than this, Priscilla." He looked over her haggard frame. Mox wanted to cry.

"You always told me I was strong, Mox, but this shit is stronger." She admitted.

A curly haired little girl tugged at Priscilla's sleeve. "Mommy, I want a present." She pressed.

"Is that your daughter?"

"Yes, and she's gettin' on my last nerve about these damn toys."

Mox kneeled down in front of the little girl. "She's gorgeous Priscilla. Hi there, beautiful. What's your name?" he inquired.

The little girl smiled and answered. "Brandi."

"Hi Brandi, my name is Mox and me and your mom are very good friends. Let me ask you something, Brandi. If there was one toy you could have in the whole world...what would it be?"

With no hesitation, Brandi shouted, "Dora!"

Mox couldn't help but to laugh at her glee, but he didn't have a clue what Dora was.

"Ok, what's Dora?" Brandi pointed to a three foot doll sitting on the back of the truck. "Oh, that's Dora, well let's go get her." Mox grabbed Brandi's hand and led her through the sea of children while Priscilla followed. He yelled for one of the helpers to get the doll.

"Mox, you don't have to do this."

"Yes I do. Here you go, Brandi." He sat the doll right next to her.

"Thank you." She said.

Mox watched her eyes shine and her lips curl into a smile. This is what life was about; being able to have a hand in someone else's happiness. Mox enjoyed these very moments.

Priscilla looked at Mox. "Why do you do this?"

"Because if I don't, who will? I sold a lot of drugs out here, you know how it was. I took away from plenty of mouths and destroyed more than enough families pushing work through here." Mox reflected. "I'm in a position now that I'm able to give back to the people that gave to me, so it's only right."

Priscilla eyed Mox. “What about us, Mox?

In the back of his mind he was thinking the same thing. He and Priscilla had a past that was so strong, the energy could still be felt.

He and Priscilla met when Mox was 15 and she was 18. She loved her some Mox and at the time, she was ready to do any and everything he asked.

Unbeknownst to Mox, Priscilla was a few weeks pregnant when he went on the run. Nine months later, she pushed out a 7 pound, 5 ounce baby girl and named her Brandi.

Priscilla did all she could to contact Mox, but he cut his ties to the outside world when he became a fugitive. She even went as far as finding his whereabouts through the internet and writing letters to him while he was incarcerated, but she never received a response.

A few years passed, and Priscilla became involved with one of her younger brother's friends named Ryan.

Ryan was a fairly decent, local cocaine dealer. He was seeing a few stacks a week and Priscilla preyed on his weakness of lust. She let him let him taste the pink candy and had him wrapped up like a car wreck on the interstate from that day forward.

Ryan was in to popping pills heavy while he and Priscilla were together. One night he convinced Priscilla to take a double stack ecstasy pill with him after she had been complaining about being stressed out. In a time span of less than ninety days Priscilla had become addicted to hard core drugs. There weren't many that she hadn't tried, but ultimately her drug of choice became cocaine.

"I don't know, Priscilla. I guess we both went our separate ways."

"No, Mox...you left me. You left me sittin' in a fuckin' parking lot." She stated.

"I ran because I was scared, Priscilla."

"Scared of what?”

“Of losing you. I didn't wanna go in there and be stressed out worrying about what you doing, so I cut all ties. I felt it was something I needed to do in order to get through that situation.”

“And how long ago was that? It's been more than five years, Mox."

"You right, but I don't know what you want me to tell you."

"You don't have to tell me anything." She announced, grabbing the child's arm. "At least say goodbye to your daughter. C'mon, Brandi, we're leaving."

Mox brushed her words off. "Don’t lie like that, Priscilla."

"Lie? No Mox I'm not lying. Look at her eyes, familiar huh?"

He kneeled down to get a better view and right away his knees got weak. He stared, and Brandi smiled. Her eyes were rare and he knew because his were the same.

The color is true brown amber which is a very uncommon color in human beings. They have a brownish, yellow tint and they're uniquely wolf like.

Brandi's eyes were identical to his.

Mox stood up and tried to take a moment to think, but Priscilla was persistent

"Oh, and if that ain't enough... come here, Brandi." She unwrapped the scarf from around her neck. "What's that right there?" she pointed to Brandi's star shaped birthmark at the top of her back.
Mox felt electricity shoot through his body. It was the same birthmark he had in the exact same location. He started sweating and it was thirty two degrees outside. He couldn't take his eyes off Brandi. He remembered the last night he

and Priscilla were together, now all of a sudden it seemed like yesterday.

Mox reached out to touch Brandi's shoulder and she lunged into his arms. He held her close and tight and then he turned to look at Priscilla, and she was gone.

ELEVEN

Almost a week passed and Mox still hadn't found Priscilla. He had no number, no address and not a clue of where she would be. *How could a parent abandon their child?* He thought, but the irony was that he had done the exact same thing.

Vegas was hours away, and Mox had a new found duty as a father; to raise his child. If that was the case, he would have no problem stepping up, but his lifestyle was dangerous and the last thing he wanted to do was put his baby girl in harm's way.

"How you know she's yours?"

"You saw her, Cleo. She looks just like me."

Cleo grabbed a few chips out the bag that was sitting on the table and stuffed them in his mouth. "I wouldn't trust no fiend."

"Priscilla aint no fiend, she's just going through somethin' right now. I know her."

"You know her?"

"Yeah, I know her." Mox got defensive.

Cleo could see he was getting under his skin. "So, how you gon' handle this? I mean, a little girl is big responsibility."

"I know, Cleo," Mox said, rubbing his temples. The stress of the situation was setting in and he didn't know how to deal with it. "The fucked up part is; she hasn't mentioned her mother yet."

"That should tell you something. Her mother probably don't give a fuck."

Mox was fed up. "I don't need your negative feedback, Cleo. Keep your opinion to yourself."

Mox glanced over at Brandi sound asleep on the couch. Every time he looked at her he saw more of himself. It was surprising and astounding at the same time.

Their flight to Vegas was departing in less than three hours and he was hoping Cleo's girl, Susan would watch after Brandi while they were gone. At first thought, Mox was a bit skeptical on leaving his child with a stranger, but after reasoning, Cleo convinced him.

Susan had mocha skin, full lips, round hips and big hair. She owned a brownstone on 138th and Amsterdam Avenue in Harlem. She also had an eight year old daughter who looked to be well taken care of, so Mox felt at ease.

"I didn't know you had a daughter, Mox?" Susan said, taking a seat next to Brandi."

"Me either." He laughed. "Susan, you sure it won't be a problem leaving her here?"

"Mox, how many times am I going to tell you, it's ok, besides, my daughter will be home in the morning so she'll have someone to play with. Trust me, she's good."

Mox looked around at the stylish home, he was impressed. You can tell a lot about a person's character as soon as you step through the door to their house and he knew Cleo wouldn't recommend someone who wasn't trustworthy. He just had that brand new father jitters.

Two and a half hours later Cleo and Mox were on a flight to Vegas.

The plane landed at McCarran International on Wayne Newton Blvd.

Mox and Cleo jumped into a limo and headed to the Palazzo hotel. As usual, Cleo wasted no time hitting the casino while Mox went and checked into his room. He had a lot on his mind. A war with the Italians was slowly brewing and making the wrong move could lead to a disastrous ending for them all.

He spent the rest of the night thinking about his daughter and drinking his pains away. By the time the sun rose, he was ready to see what the Italians had to say.

One by one, each Union delegate entered the large conference room and took a seat. Mikey and Vito sat at one end of the oak table while Cleo and Mox sat at the other. The remaining four Reps sat in twos on each side and Tommy, Mikey and Vito's cousin, stood off to the side.

Tommy was ordered by The Old Man to escort Mikey and Vito to the meeting just in case things got out of hand. Tommy stood 6 ft. 5 inches and had to weigh in at a good 290 pounds. His gorilla likes features made him hard to look at and his scowl was always minacious.

Mikey stood to talk. "Greetings, gentlemen... due to a family situation, The Old Man will not be joining us today, so Vito and I will be speaking on his behalf."

Everyone nodded their head in recognition except for Mox.

Slumped in his chair, sporting a three thousand dollar suit, he blew smoke clouds into the air. "So, you the boss now?" he said, sarcastically.

Mikey smiled and sat back down.

"Mox, let me handle this," Cleo interrupted.

"Good morning, delegates. As you all know, this is the first meeting of the year, so happy New Year to you and your families. Next, nothing has changed as far as Union dues so let's get that out the way first."

At the start of the meeting each Union Rep is responsible for their monthly Union fees. The fee amount varies between boroughs and the total amount is then split between Mox, Cleo and the Italians.

Each Rep opened up a briefcase, said their total amount and emptied the contents into a bag that sat atop the table. It totaled $700,000 cash.

Mikey rose from his seat to address the Union. "Mox, I think I deserve a thank you."

"A thank you? For what?"

"For lettin' you breathe. Only off the strength of Cleo are you still alive."

"Suck a dick, Mikey. If you wanna go to war, fuck it, let's go to war."

Cleo jumped in. "Hold up guys, nobody's going to war here. It's too much money involved."

"Well, put a leash on your dog, Cleo." Vito barked. "He's way outta line."

"No, you're outta line, Vito. I didn't start this shit, you did." Mox replied.

"It doesn't matter who started what. We got a problem and we need to get it solved here and now." Cleo said.

"Cleo, you know I got respect for you as well as every other man sitting at this table," Mikey stated. "But the disrespect will no longer be tolerated; let's not forget who brought you in this."

"So, what are you saying, Mikey?"

"I said it, Cleo. What I say goes. My father started you guys in this business and I'll be damned if I let your hot headed cousin screw it up."

Mox's anger increased. "You gon' let him talk to you like that, Cleo?"

"Cleo's not the problem Mox, it's you!" Vito shouted.

Mikey walked over to the opposite end of the table and immediately Mox stood in defense. Their eyes locked.

Tommy stood still in the back with his chest pumped.

"If you gon' make a move, Mikey it better be a good one. Remember, we playing chess here, not checkers." Mox reminded.

Vito sat in his chair snickering. "Well, it looks to me like you're playing without your Queen." he teased.

Mox thought about pulling his weapon and shooting Vito between the eyes, but that wouldn't be enough for him. He wanted to make them feel the pain and anguish he was feeling.

"You know the body aint worth shit without the head, right?" Mox hinted.

Vito's face instantly turned red. Nobody threatened a Telesco and got away with it. "You got some fuckin' nerve, Mox. Are you making threats now?"

"Gentlemen," Cleo intervened. "This is going nowhere; all the bickering back and forth ain't solving the problem. We're here to discuss business and all I hear is bitching.

"You right, Cleo. That Queens issue hasn't been resolved yet either," Mox said.

"You still talkin' about Queens?" Mikey replied. "Nobody's touchin' Queens, that's that."

Cleo sensed the frustration. "Fair is fair, Mikey. We had an agreement and you guys broke it."

"Queens was never part of the deal," Vito chimed.

Mox slowly shook his head and turned his wolf like eyes up to his cousin. "You see how they treat us, Cleo..." he paused and looked each man at the table in their eyes. "You trust these muthafuckas?"

Cleo didn't respond immediately, he just stared. Then he said, "Yeah, I trust 'em."

"Well, I don't!" Mox raised his nine with the swiftness and precision of a firearm specialist. Simultaneously each Rep stood with their guns pointed at the Italians.

Tommy reached to draw his weapon, but it was too late.

Mox held his gun firm and approached Vito who was still sitting, scared to death. "Talk that tough guy shit now, Vito."

Mikey kept his cool. "Mox, you making a big mistake."

"Oh, yeah. Well we all sometimes make mistakes. What counts is how we deal with the consequences."

"Mox! What the fuck are you doing?!"

"Cleo, chill. I got this. Papi! Get the bag, we out."

Mox cocked his gun and put it to Vito's kneecap while Papi grabbed the bag of money. He could smell the parmesan cheese on his breath from his heavy breathing.

He sensed the fear.

Mikey tried to move, but Nate snatched his arm and shoved a pistol to his neck.

On the other side, Javier and Frank held Tommy at bay.

“Don’t do this, Mox!” Cleo urged.

Mox looked at Cleo then over to Mikey. His smile turned poisonous seconds before he choked the trigger and blew Vito’s kneecap to shreds.

The violent squall could be heard throughout the entire top floor.

Mikey watched in rage as his little brother begged for his life. “You muthafucker!” he shrieked.

Vito fell to the floor, blood spilling from his wound. He had never been shot before, the pain was grueling.

Mox turned to leave, but glanced back at Cleo. "You coming or not?"

Cleo never answered; he just stood up and walked out.

"You think you gonna get away with this shit, Cleo!" Mikey yelled. "I'm gonna fuckin' bury you!"

"Hey, Mikey... tell The Old Man I said grazie!" (Thank You) Mox joked.

Mox's plan wasn't to go to Vegas and shoot Vito, but after they killed Kim he was acting on emotion. He had love for Kim, for real.

Knowing Cleo wouldn't agree with his original idea, which was to take the Union fees, he promised the Reps a percentage of the total amount if they agreed to hold him down.

Before shooting Vito, Mox carefully weighed his options. In his heart, he felt he could not only handle a war with the Italians, but win in the process. All he needed was to get Cleo to see things the way he did.

Feathery snow flurries fell from the sky, blanketing the concrete as the 25 mph winds raked the naked trees and ripped its branches.

A shiny, black Town car came to a complete stop directly across the street from the projects and Cleo stepped out.

"Meet me back here in one hour, Chris." He instructed.

Two whole days had passed since the Vegas episode and Cleo hadn't spoken to Mox yet. He was considerably upset and wanted an explanation at once. His ties with the Italians were sure to be severed completely, and even more than that he now had to keep a close watch of his surroundings and move about cautiously.

Cleo hustled down the wintry strip and into building 60. The overpowering stench of weed, urine and cigarette smoke filled his nostrils upon entry. He stepped onto the pitch black elevator and hit the button to go to the sixth floor. When the door opened, Cleo went right to apartment 6H and knocked loudly.

Inside the apartment, Dana scurried to the back room to warn Mox that someone was at the door.

"Shh..." He put his index finger to his lips and removed his weapon from his waistline. "Go get Brandi and bring her back here." he whispered.

Dana was Mox's best friend growing up. She stood 5'9, mahogany brown skin, sexy heart shaped lips, thick thighs and a firm ass from her dedicated 3-days-a week workout plan. She was well educated, and more than likely the only female he actually slept in a bed with and never once pursued sex. They had a mutual respect for each other and Dana only wanted to see Mox prosper.

Back when they were younger, he would run over to her building and knock on her door after he got a beating. He stood there each time with dried up tears on his cheek, snot falling from his nostrils and the saddest frown you ever saw. Dana had no choice but to let him in because she knew all he wanted was some of her mother's chocolate chip cookies. She felt bad for Mox. She really liked him as a friend and was one of the few who saw with her own eyes, the struggle he was going through.

She tip-toed to the front, grabbed Brandi and walked her to the back while Mox went to see who was knocking. He glimpsed through the peephole and recognized Cleo standing there with a face full of frustration.

The door opened, and Cleo's eyes fell on the gun Mox held in his left hand. "I don't think killers knock on the door," he teased.

"The last one did." Mox clarified. He peered in to the hallway to make sure no one else was there. "What's good cousin? I knew you'd be coming around sooner or later."

Cleo shook his head with resentment and entered the apartment. “That shit you pulled in Vegas gon’ get us killed for sure. What the fuck is wrong wit’ you, Mox?”

“Keep your voice down Cleo, Brandi and Dana in the back room.”

“Mox, you don’t get it. You initiated a war with the Italians. This shit is serious.”

“It ain’t no more serious than going to war with niggas on the block Cleo, don’t tell me you scared of these dudes?”

“It’s not about being scared. It’s about being smart and making the best suitable decision,” Cleo reasoned.

“The best suitable decision?” He repeated. “Listen cousin. Our original agreement with the Italians was twenty percent of everything with the possibility of an increase upon us driving the numbers up. Now tell me if I’m wrong, but from day one until now... those numbers are up and always have been.” Mox sat in the fold up chair next to the sofa and fronted Cleo. “These bastards making millions off us, Cleo and all we eating is scraps off the fuckin’ table!”

“You greedy Mox.”

"I'm not greedy. I'm hungry. You saw that little girl. Aint no denying that, Cleo That's my reality and I gotta handle that, so this shit aint even about me no more."

Mox got up from his seat and sat next to Cleo on the sofa. "I got too much love for you to let a nigga hurt you. You know that. We family, nigga and right now I need you."

"I don't know, Mox."

"Hold up. I'll be right back." Mox got up and went to the bedroom. He came out with the bag from Vegas. "I got three hundred stacks in here and half is yours. I hit Nate, Javier, Frank and Papi off with a hundred a piece, so everybody is good."

Cleo gazed down at the bag full of money. One hundred and fifty thousand was much better than the usual twenty percent they got, but it came at a heavy price that he wasn't willing to pay.

"You had this planned out already, huh?"

Mox smirked. "Not really. I aint gon' lie, I was gon' take that bread, but then they killed my girl, Cleo. I had to make somebody bleed."

"I don't think you understand what you getting yourself in to."

Mox carefully listened to Cleo's words. "So, you don't want none of this?" He asked, ruffling through the stacks of bills."

Cleo got up from the sofa and gestured to make his exit. "We can't win this one, Mox. Sometimes you gotta know when to bow out."

"I ain't bowing down to nobody, fuck them Italians!" Mox hissed. "You go over there and try to talk to them muthafuckas and they gon' blow your head off. They don't give a fuck about you Cleo, you just another nigga. Do you really think Mikey gon' ride with you before he ride with his family?"

"I knew Mikey since we were kids." Cleo reasoned, opening the front door.

"Oh, so what that mean, you think he won't kill you, Cleo? The Union, Cleo; No-one stands before WE!" Mox yelled as Cleo walked out.

TWELVE

Downtown - Brooklyn, New York

The stoplight at Hoyt and Atlantic was temporarily out of order and traffic was becoming extremely congested. Horns blared and irritated motorists complained aloud about the chaos on the roads.

Javier clenched the steering wheel and mashed his foot on the brake to avoid smashing into the vehicle two feet in front of him. “Watch where the fuck you going!” he shouted. He slowly eased up to where the traffic officer stood trying to direct the gridlock.

The officer gestured for him stop and approached the driver’s side window. “License and registration" he ordered.

“You just let ten people go pass and now you wanna pull me over? This is crazy.”

Javier was furious. He couldn't understand why he was the only one getting pulled over. He reached for his wallet and gave the officer his license and then he popped the glove compartment open and searched for the registration. He felt the small .380 underneath some papers.

"You're kinda young to be driving an eighty thousand dollar car. What type of work you do?"

Javier twisted his neck and gave the officer his best screw face. He hated cops, black and white. He was ready to shoot him and pull off, but the traffic was even more backed up now.

"I sell cars." He answered. And he wasn't lying either, but the whole truth was, the cars are stolen.

"Oh, yeah... what kind?"

Javier's hand eased off the pistol. "All types, they're used, here, take a card." he pulled a business card from the middle console and handed it to the cop.

"Javier's Auto" He read out loud. "That's cool. Here you go." the officer gave Javier his license back and let him pass.

The glare from the sunlight was in his eyes so he pulled the sun visor down, made the right onto Atlantic and ran into some more traffic.

“Shit!” He hit the Bluetooth button and spoke to the system. “Call Rene.” he said slowly and clearly so he could be heard. After a few rings a sexy, female voice came through the speakers.

“What’s up, baby?”

“Rene, I’ma be there in like a half hour.”

“A half hour?... Nigaa my pussy wet right now. You playing games, Javier. I swear I hate fuckin’ wit you.”

Javier smiled “Oh, word?” He was feeling himself. He knew every time she said that, she meant the exact opposite.

He saw an open in the lane next to him, stepped on the gas and turned the wheel quickly. The Town car behind him was coming too fast and smashed the rear of his new Audi.

Javier’s body jerked and he was pushed forward into the steering wheel. “Oh, shit!”

“Hello?”

He grabbed the back of his neck and grimaced. “Somebody just crashed in to the back of my shit.” He grumbled.

“You alright?”

He turned to look out the back window and caught site of the two, dark suited, gun toting, white men moving in quick.

His survival instincts immediately kicked in and he got as low as he could, opened the glove compartment and snatched the gun. He raised his arm and blindly let off three shots through the back windshield, dropping one of the dark suits.

The traffic officer around the corner heard the shots and radioed for back up and at the same time a blue and white NYPD patrol car was cruising Atlantic on the opposite side where traffic was at a minimum. Hearing the shots, he sped up to where the accident was and jumped out the vehicle with his gun drawn.

The other dark suit fired the fully automatic machine gun he held in his hands and bullets ripped through windshields striking innocent bystanders as they sat in the backed up traffic.

Javier hit the clutch, shifted gears and smashed his foot on the gas pedal.

The cop's gun was blaring and sirens howled in the background. He turned the wheel and tried to maneuver his way out, but only got fifty feet before crashing into a delivery van.

The gunfire was loud and continuous as Javier staggered from the wrecked automobile. He felt his left arm go numb and when he looked down he saw blood leaking from a hole in his shoulder. There was no time to worry about that because dark suit's gun was still spitting out rounds.

After he dropped one officer, the dark suited gunman turned and fired on the traffic cop who was ducking behind cars trying to shield himself. This gave Javier a few seconds to execute his next move.

He hobbled to a grey, Toyota Camry that was twenty five feet in front of him and tugged at the door handle. It was locked. The driver, an elderly white woman, was slumped in her seat with a bullet hole in the back of her head.

Javier smashed the driver's side window with the gun in his hand and opened the door. He yanked the dead woman's limp body from the seat, tossed her to the ground, jumped behind the wheel and escaped the lurid scene with minimal damage.

It was 9:30 pm and the projects were a ghost town. Except for a few stray cats and a junkie here and there, Ryan was the only one out, huddled in the cut on the side of building 80.

He let the smoke flow through his nostrils and plucked the clip of marijuana into the grass. When he looked up, he saw a common face approaching.

From a distance he nodded and she nodded back.

“What’s up, what you want?”

“Please, Ryan, jus gimme two for thirty-five this one time. You know I always come straight.”

“I don’t take short money. Look at these shits.” Ryan bragged. “This is the best shit out here.” he held two clear, glassine baggies filled with cocaine in his palm.

Priscilla's eyes enlarged at the sight of the irresistible drug. She grew extremely eager and her mouth twitched. "C'mon, Ryan, I'll bring it back. I swear."

He tucked the drugs back into his pants pocket. "I heard that lie a thousand times, Priscilla. You full of shit. Get the fuck outta my face."

Apprehensive and jittery, she crammed her hands back into her pockets hoping some money would magically materialize. She felt something, dug deeper and pulled out a brand new pair of diamond studded earrings.

"Look. I got these!" She bellowed and shoved the two, half karat stones in his face.

"Let me see those." Ryan grabbed Priscilla's wrist, twisted it and dumped the rocks into his hand. He eyed the beautiful nuggets and then he looked at Priscilla and shook his head. He opted to just turn around and walk off, but his feelings were hurt by her actions.

Ryan put the earrings in his pocket.

Priscilla smiled. "Ok, so what you gon' gimmie for 'em?"

"What I'ma give you for 'em?" He reached into his sweat pants and backed out a chrome .45 ACP with black plastic on the handle.

Priscilla was stumped. She didn't have a clue of what was going on and she had never saw Ryan with so much disgust in his eyes. "What are you doing, Ryan?" she panicked.

The strike was immediate. As soon as the butt of the gun touched her face, blood shot from her nose. She folded, fell to the ground and Ryan stepped back, raised his leg and kicked her in the stomach while she was down.

"You stupid, bitch! I bought these earrings for Brandi's second birthday! You sniffin' that much fuckin' coke, huh!?" He was steamed. He stood over Priscilla as she fought to get back to her feet.

"Ryan, I'm sorry..." She sobbed. Blood was trickling from her nose like a leaky, project faucet. She touched her face and scowled. Her nose was broken. She could feel it.

Ryan cocked his right hand and struck her in the abdomen with a ruthless blow, sending her back to the pavement in agony.

"You out here twisted. Get your shit together, Priscilla!" He said, and strutted up the empty project strip.

Priscilla bled on the freezing concrete. Eyes closed. Envisioning a life she always dreamt about, a life she once lived. She thought about her daughter and all the people she wronged. Knowing she was better than what the world saw, Priscilla promised herself she would listen to Ryan for the first time and really get her shit together. It was a must.

Cleo lounged in the backseat of the cab fidgeting with his new phone. "Chris, wassup... you don't seem like yourself today. Is something bothering you?"

Chris kept his hands on the wheel and his eyes on the road. Something was troubling him, but he didn't want to burden Cleo with his problems, so he downplayed it.

"You know; regular problems with my girl, nothing crazy."

Cleo knew he wasn't telling it all, but it was his business and if he didn't want to share it, that was fine too. "Ok... yea, I got those problems too."

They both laughed.

Cleo's phone rang and it surprised him. He couldn't figure out how someone had already gotten his new number. He only had the phone for two days.

"Hello?"

The caller hung up.

"They starting this shit already." He whispered. Cleo looked up and noticed they had been sitting at the light for longer than usual. "Wassup with this light Chris?"

He looked up at the light. "I don't know, Cleo. Maybe it's broken."

Suddenly the backside passenger door swung open and Vito grilled Cleo with a six shot .38 in his hand and one knee wrapped in gauze. "Get in the car."

Cleo spun his head.

The other door came open and a short, fat, slick haired white guy had a twelve gage shotgun pointed at his chest.

"I aint going nowhere."

A black Town car pulled up to the open door and the back window came down.

“Hey, Cleo. Get in the fuckin’ car!” The Old man hollered.

Seeing how serious he was, Cleo complied. He tapped Chris’ headrest. “Go head, I’m good from here.” he slowly exited the cab and entered the black Town car with the Mafia Boss. Vinny Telesco.

Chris never looked back. He pressed on the gas, went through the light and continued to the highway.

Another Town car pulled up and Vito limped to the backseat. The slick haired, fat guy jumped in the front seat of Vinny’s car and they peeled off.

Cleo looked out the window at the passing scenery. He paid no attention to The Old Man.

“You can’t even look me in my face, Cleo.”

“It wasn’t my fault, Vinny.” He tried to explain.

“The fuck if it wasn’t your fault. He’s been your responsibility from day one.” The Old Man wheezed. “You vouched for him Cleo. If I didn’t like you, I’d have Sammy the scar up there put a few in the back of your fuckin’ head.”

Sammy turned in his seat and smiled. The sight of his discolored, rotten teeth made Cleo's lip curl. "Turn the fuck around, Sammy... I aint talking to you."

"Just give me some time Vinny, I'll take care of it." Cleo lied.

"Time's runnin' out. I'm giving you one chance and one chance only. I don't wanna hear any more about Mox."

It took him a minute, but soon enough, Cleo finally caught on to what The Old Man was trying to say. He couldn't believe what he was being asked to do.

Cleo looked at the Mafia Boss for the first time since he'd been forced into the car.

"I can't do that, Vinny." he pleaded.

The Old Man rubbed his hands together, loosened his tie and fixed his beady eyes on Cleo. "It's either blood on your hands or dirt on your grave. Whichever one you choose, Cleo." he hit the button to let the window down and a cool breeze caressed his face. "Jimmy, pull over." he instructed. "Now get the fuck outta my car."
Cleo wanted to tell The Old Man to fuck off, but he was smarter than that and being ignorant in this situation was

only going to lead to one outcome; a casket. One thing was for sure, he wasn't taking orders from nobody. He was going to handle the situation however he saw fit. Fuck the Telesco's.

He stepped out the car and noticed that he was on the side of the highway in between Mt. Vernon and the Bronx, so he reached for his cell phone and made a call.

"Wassup, Cleo?" A voice on the other end answered.

"It's time to earn your stripes, young nigga." He hit end.

THIRTEEN

Thick blackish clouds hung in the air, creating a dull setting to the mornings rise as Mox hesitated to get up from his warm bed and start the day. He stretched and made an attempt to push the heinous visions of reoccurring nightmares from his head. Since witnessing the murder of his parents, a good night's sleep was almost impossible.

He stepped into his slippers, tossed his silk robe onto his back and went to check on Brandi in the guest room down the hall. When he opened the door, she was sitting upright watching Dora the Explorer on the 40 inch flat screen in front of the bed.

"Good morning, beautiful." He poked his head through the door.

She giggled at his playful antics and replied, "Good morning."

"You know what today is, right?"

Brandi quickly hopped off the bed and jumped into Mox's arms. "Surprise Saturday!" she yelled.

For the past two weekends Mox would have a gift delivered to the house for Brandi to celebrate Surprise Saturday. It was an idea he came up with after he realized how life was for her growing up with a parent on drugs. He'd gone through the same thing.

Suddenly, a sharp flash of light lit the entire room followed by a rumbling thunder. Torrential rains fell from the dark skies and violent winds ripped branches from the trees.

Immediately, Brandi threw her arms around Mox's neck and held on with all her strength. Her face was buried in his chest.

"Daddy, I'm scared." She sobbed.

Mox held her tightly. He brushed her hair back with his hand. "Don't be scared, baby it's just some thunder and lightning."

"I know, but I don't like it."

Mox smiled, "Me either." he turned and carried Brandi down the steps and into the kitchen. "What you want to eat this morning?" he asked.

Every morning, Mox would wake up and make Brandi anything she wanted for breakfast. His cooking was decent too.

"I want pancakes, eggs and umm..." She thought hard. "Oh, bacon!"

"Pancakes, eggs and turkey bacon, coming up."

Another growl roared through the skies and this time the lightning seemed like it was closer. Brandi rushed from the table and attached herself to Mox's leg as he gathered the utensils to cook.

"I got you, baby. Don't worry." Mox kept her by his side while he cooked their breakfast.

As they sat and ate, the severe downpour continued. Mox laughed and watched Brandi drown her pancakes in syrup.

"Daddy, is that God?"

"Is who God?"

"Whoever is making all that noise and rain."

He smiled. "I'm sure he has a lot to do with it."

"How does he make those loud noises?"

Mox sat upright in his seat and wiped his mouth with a napkin. He loved when Brandi asked questions. It showed that she was curious about the things going on around her. He thought about her latest and tried to explain it the best way he could.

"Alright. You listening?" She said yes. "Now, when warm air rises it mixes with the cool air. Up there." he pointed. "When they get mixed together they form a cloud. The cloud keeps rising into the air and raindrops form inside and they start falling from the cloud. Now, when the cloud reaches a certain height that's when we have thunderstorms. They're called cumulonimbus clouds."

Brandi dropped her fork on the plate. "Huh?"

Mox laughed hard. "Alright. I'll teach that word later. C'mon lets go put a movie on until the delivery guy comes." They got up from the kitchen table and walked into the plush living room.

Mox's lair was a bachelor's dream pad. Gorgeous carpets and hand placed tiles covered almost every square inch of the estate. He and Brandi got comfortable on the fine, imported, French leather chaise lounge and watched *Diary of a Wimpy Kid* on the 200 inch projection screen until they both fell asleep.

Forty-five minutes later, the vibration of Mox's cell phone on the glass, coffee table awoke him. He glanced at it and then looked at Brandi. She was in a deep sleep.

"Mox, I need to come and talk to you." The caller said.

"You know where I'm at."

"Cool, I'll be through in a minute."

Mox relaxed into a deep nap and when he got up the clock read 4:25 pm. He and Brandi had slept the entire day away.

He tapped her shoulder to wake her up and realized Gene; the delivery man hadn't arrived yet. It was a bit unusual because he always made his deliveries before 3pm on Saturdays.

Mox walked Brandi upstairs to the master bathroom and the doorbell rang. His natural instinct was to look up at one of the 25 camera's he had placed throughout the house, but he remembered the system had been down for the past few weeks.

“Go use the bathroom. This might be the delivery man.” He told her and rushed down the hall to his bedroom.

He sneakily pulled the curtain back and saw the dark colored delivery truck parked in front of his driveway. Some of his tension was eased at the sight of the well-known vehicle.

Mox snatched the .357 Sig off his dresser on the way downstairs. He definitely wasn’t about to get caught slipping.

“Brandi. You alright in there?” He stopped in front of the bathroom, tucked the weapon in the small of his back and let his t-shirt cover it.

Brandi yelled. “Yes! I’m okay!”

“Alright, let me know when you’re done.”

The bell rang again as Mox hurried down the steps to the front door. “I’m coming, Gene.” he turned the knob. “You a little late to—”

The barrel of a shotgun was gawking at Mox’s chest and before he got to finish his sentence, the explosive blast sent him flying to the floor.

By the grace of God he only caught a few pellets in the abdomen. He rolled over to get from in range of the next discharge and the slug ripped the expensive floor tiles to crumbs.

He reached for the Sig tucked in his pants, but he didn't feel it. He panicked slightly and then scoured the area. It was lying on the floor about ten feet away and must have come out of his pants when he hit the ground.

Mox rolled across the floor like he was on fire and made it to the gun. He palmed it and dashed to the steps where he finally got a few seconds to think while the gunman reloaded.

At first he didn't recognize the shooter, but then he saw the man sent to take his life was Tommy Telesco.

Mox made it to the bathroom door and called out for his daughter. "Brandi! You still in there?"

"Yes daddy. I'm scared. The thunder is getting louder."

He touched his side and immediately his hand was covered in blood. The wound was burning. "Stay in there until I tell you to come out, alright?"

"Okay, but I'm done." She said.

"Just lock the door and get in the tub."

Brandi did as she was told.

Meanwhile, Tommy crept up the steps with destruction in his eyes and fresh slugs loaded into his weapon. Ready to fulfill the order he was given.

He raised the shotgun, plucked the trigger and the blast tore away chunks of the hand crafted, wooden banister.

Mox ducked and shielded himself from shards of debris in the air. His opportunity came and he let the barrel fly, tossing rounds through the smoke filled atmosphere.

A bullet hit Tommy's upper shoulder. He stumbled and dropped the weapon, but one bullet wasn't enough to immobilize the brawny assassin.

After he regained his balance, he picked the shotgun up, but instantly he tossed it back down after realizing he had no more slugs. He went for the small .38 revolver in the small of his back and capped off two shots, hitting nothing.

Mox inhaled. He paused and thought about his daughter. She was the only reason he had to live. He was not only willing to put his life on the line, but also prepared to take one if that's what it took to make sure nothing happened to her.

Light sweat formed in his palm as he gripped the compact cannon. He could hear Tommy's footsteps getting closer with each passing second. His timing was perfect. As soon as the Mafioso henchman rounded the corner a .357 projectile smashed into his cheek. The contact from the bullet cracked his jaw and broke his nose on impact.

Tommy went down and Mox rushed over to finish the job.

He looked at the helpless tough guy. "At a certain point in our lives we all gotta go, today just happened to be your day."

Fire shot from the nozzle of the sig and a bullet landed between Tommy's eyes. Mox didn't have to check to see if he was dead. He never second guessed his work.

The bathroom door came open and Brandi's innocent face appeared in the crack. She glanced down at the bloody giant.

Mox hurried to where she stood. "C'mon, baby we gotta get out of here." He grabbed her arm.

“But what about, Surprise Saturday?” She asked, her voice, sweet and gentle.

“I’ll make up for it.”

Mox scurried through the house with Brandi by his side. He entered his bedroom and quickly emptied the $125,000 dollars that was in his safe into a Luis Vuitton duffle bag. He checked the dresser drawer, picked up his HD camera and tossed it in the bag also.

His truck was parked at the entrance of the house, but leaving out the front door wouldn’t be the smartest decision. His other car was parked in the garage so he threw the bag over his shoulder and he and Brandi made an exit out the back of the house.

FOURTEEN

Chris turned the wheel and made the right onto Mox's block. A line of unmarked police cars filled the street and homicide detectives were combing the scene.

"I don't think you wanna go down there." Chris warned.

Cleo lifted his head and glanced out the window at the disorder. He couldn't believe what he was seeing.

"Make the U-turn, Chris. Get me outta here."

"Anywhere in particular?"

"The projects."

Six minutes later, Chris pulled the Town car over and Cleo got out and walked into the projects.

After Christmas and New Year's passed, there weren't many people wandering about in the projects. It actually resembled a ghost town.

The frosty winds kissed Cleo's cheeks and he tugged at his wool hat pulling it down over his ears. He slowly approached two young guys as they stood on the strip, engaged in a heated conversation about sports.

"Man, fuck Kobe. That nigga's a snitch!" Tyrell shouted. The kid he was talking to shook his head and kept his mouth shut. He knew how Tyrell got when he became angry.

"Youngin, wassup?" Cleo interrupted.

Tyrell stepped away from his conversation and greeted Cleo with a handshake.

"You tell me, boss. I was out here all night waitin' for you."

"What I tell you about that boss shit."

"My bad. Jus' tryna show respect. That's all."

Tyrell Michaels, the gullible sixteen year old, would do anything to get a name in the hood. He had a few shootings under his belt, but for the most part he was a low level hustler looking for a come up.

Every now and then, Cleo would come through the hood and drop some work off for Tyrell and his team to move. It was never anything too big, a few ounces of weed maybe a couple hundred grams of coke. It was more than enough to put Tyrell on, but all he wanted was a rental car for the month, some new gear, and all the weed he could smoke.

Cleo whispered in Tyrell's ear. "Did Mox come through here?"

Tyrell nodded toward the building. "He's upstairs." He told the kid he was talking to that he would see him later and him and Cleo walked into the building.

They exited the elevator on the sixth floor and Cleo knocked on Dana's door.

"Who is it?" She yelled.

Cleo gestured for Tyrell to say his name.

"It's me, Tyrell."

The door swung open and the two men entered the apartment.

Dana was barely dressed in a tank top and a pair of tight fitting shorts that accentuated her ass cheeks and made her camel toe obviously visible. She had light beads of sweat sitting on her forehead, her hair was pin wrapped and she was breathing kind of fast.

“Fuck you in here doin’… workin’ out?” Tyrell joked, but his guess was right. A workout DVD was playing on the 30 inch television.

Dana slammed the door shut and locked it after they came in.

“Damn, Tyrell. Do you ever go to school?” She asked.

He brushed past her and took a seat on the sofa. “I can’t get money in school.”

“Maybe not, but you can get a fuckin’ education. Duh.” She sassed, rolling her eyes at her little cousin. “Wassup, Cleo? Mox is in the back.”

“How you doin’ Dana? Can you tell him I’m out here, please?”

“Sure.”

Dana went to get Mox and Cleo grabbed the fold up chair that was against the wall. He took a seat next to the sofa.

"Yo," He whispered. "I hope you don't be tellin' Mox about our business?"

Tyrell straightened up and looked at Cleo. "Nah. Hell no." he shook his head. "Mox be on his bullshit. Him and my cousin always talkin' that school shit. Fuck that. I ain't tryna go to school, I'm tryna get this money."

Cleo smiled and nodded his head. He knew Tyrell could be manipulated easily and he planned to take advantage of his weakness.

"Aight, cool. Keep this low." He reached into his bubble coat and passed Tyrell a brown bag. "That's 200 soft and three zones of sour." Cleo lifted his coat and grabbed the gun off his waist. He cocked it and placed it on the small, wooden coffee table. "Have that next week, you heard?"

Tyrell smirked at Cleo and agreed. "I got you."

When Tyrell looked up, Mox was coming down the hall. He was shirtless with gauze wrapped around his mid-section.

Tyrell raised his eyebrows twice to inform Cleo.

"Why you aint in school?" Mox questioned, as he entered the living room.

Tyrell sighed and glanced at Cleo. "See." he picked the remote control up and hit the power button. "Mox, I don't wanna go to school. Let me hold somethin'?"

Mox told Tyrell to move over so he could sit on the sofa directly across from Cleo. He snatched the remote out of his hand and changed the channel.

"You running wit' young niggas now, Cleo?" He picked the gun up off the table and turned to Tyrell. "This you?"

"Nah, that's mine." Cleo reached for the weapon, but Mox pulled away.

"Tyrell, give us a minute, please."

With no hesitation Tyrell rose from the sofa. He picked up his coat and went to leave.

"Aight, Mox... lata, Cleo."

The door shut and Mox cocked the barrel back on the handgun. He saw a bullet was loaded in the head. He dumped it on the carpet and then he hit a button and a full clip fell out the bottom.

“What’s good, Cleo?” He placed the empty weapon back on the table.

Cleo smirked. “You tell me. I went by the crib, shit was crazy. You alright?”

Mox got up and went into the kitchen a few feet away. He snatched a bottle of champagne from the fridge and picked up the ashtray with a fresh cigar in it.

“Yeah, I’m good, but before I get in to that, wassup wit’ you and that young nigga, I hope you ain’t the one giving him work?”

Cleo looked Mox in his eyes and told a blatant lie. “I aint never gave that little nigga nothin’.”

Mox didn’t believe him, but he let it ride. “Okay, so we on the same page as far as that goes,” Mox popped the top off the bottle of champagne. “Now, this other thing... this shit just went to the next level.”

“I told you to let me take care of it, I knew this shit was gon’ get outta hand.”

"It's too late for that, Cleo. Don't you understand... they came to house... while my daughter was there, what would you do?"

"I wouldn't have put myself in a situation like that in the first place."

Mox got up and went over to where Cleo sat. "You been on some real bullshit these past few weeks. What's good wit' you?"

"You don't listen, Mox. And when you don't listen that's when I get put in a fucked up position."

Mox had no problem reading between the lines. He knew just what Cleo was getting at.

"So, they sent you here to kill me?" He smiled.

Cleo kept a stern face. "Yup..."

Mox walked to the coffee table, picked the gun up and put the clip back in. Then he cocked it and held it out to Cleo. "Here's your gun... shoot me."

Cleo pushed the gun out his face. "We too strong for that Mox, cut it out. But you asked so I had to tell you the truth.

Yeah, The Old Man ordered you dead and he basically told me that I gotta be the one to do it."

"And what you tell him?"

"I didn't tell him anything, you still breathing right? I came here to let you know that I'ma ride this out wit' you. I'm loyal to family first. *Let no-one stand before WE.* Remember that?"

Mox smiled. "It took you long enough."

He still didn't fully trust his cousin's actions. There was something about Cleo's body language that made his words unbelievable and Mox detected it the last time they had a conversation, but he never jumped the gun.

Cleo relaxed in his chair. "So, what's the deal wit' Javier?"

Mox took a long swig of the champagne. "He had to get low. Two police got shot. One died; the other one still in the hospital. That shit is crazy."

"So, what's your plan now that we ain't fuckin' with the Italians. Money is gonna slow up, Mox."

"Just be cool. I got a few things I'm working on. You short, you need some paper?"

“Nah, I’m good right now.” Cleo responded.

“Listen, trust me, I’ma handle this. Our first order of business is Vinny Telesco.”

FIFTEEN

“Pop, hurry up, you’re gonna be late!” Mikey screamed as he walked out the front door.

Vinny struggled to his feet from the cozy sofa and then mumbled a few cuss words. He screwed his face up at the thought of another doctor visit. It would be the third one this week and he was growing very tired of it.

“Goddamn doctors get on my nerves, Mikey...”

“I understand pop, but ain’t nothing I can do about it. Doc says you need to come in today, says it an emergency.”

“Everything’s a fuckin’ emergency according to him.”

Mikey held the car door open while the aging, ailing Mob Boss crawled into the backseat of the limo. And then he slid in beside him.

"Jimmy, Take 87. It'll get us there faster." Vinny's voice was dry and raspy. He coughed.

"Pop, you alright?" Mikey sat up to make sure he was okay.

"Yeah, Mikey. I'm fine." He spit in his handkerchief and put it back in is coat pocket. "Where's your brother?"

"I don't know pop. He said he had something to take care of."

"Hmph..." Vinny relaxed on the fine leather and stretched his long legs in the spacious limousine. "The nerve of that guy." He was worried. "You gotta watch over him Mikey. You know Vito ain't the brightest M&M in the pack."

"Yeah, I know pop."

"Just don't let nothing happen to your brother. And what's going on with this Mox situation?"

"Not too much. I haven't heard anything from Cleo."

"He's not gonna do it. Mikey, I want you to handle that. And after Mox," Vinny looked out the window at the passing traffic. "Take care of Cleo."

"But, Pop—"

Vinny cut in. “But nothing. Just do what I tell you”

Vinny sat back in his seat, speechless. It was out of his hands. There was nothing no one could do or say.

The partition came down and Jimmy tried to get Vinny’s attention. “Excuse me, boss.”

Nobody heard him.

Mikey finally said something. “Why you so caught up on Mox, pop?”

“I got my reasons.” He answered.

Jimmy tried again. “Excuse me, boss.”

“Yeah, Jimmy.”

“I think we’re being followed.”

Mikey turned to look out the back window, but he couldn’t see out because of the dark tint. He was edgy, but Vinny kept his cool. “How far till the next exit?”

“Two miles.” Jimmy replied.

The limousine slowed up at the Central Park Avenue exit in Yonkers and the two black Mercedes 500's that were tailing did the same.

"Pull into the gas station." "Vinny ordered.

Jimmy made a right turn into the Mobile gas station and pulled over by two giant gas tanks. The only car there was getting ready to pull off.

"Mikey checked his weapon and then reached to open the door. "Let me handle this pop."

"Sit down Mikey. I can take care of myself." Vinny opened his door and stepped into a brisk, light wind that whistled at the few hairs that were left on his head. He buttoned his overcoat and watched the two 500's pull in behind him.

Jimmy removed his revolver from the glove compartment and stepped out with Vinny.

The occupants of the two Mercedes exited the vehicles, but Vinny only recognized Mox and Cleo. He had never seen the other three guys. They all donned dark, tailor fitted suits and shiny shoes.

Vinny kept his hands in his pockets while they approached. "I wasn't expecting any visitors today."

"You should always expect the unexpected, old man." Mox was standing ten feet in front of him.

"Those are quite knowledgeable words coming from a dead man." He smiled. "Cleo, I thought I asked you to do something?" Vinny studied Cleo's mannerisms. He could tell that he didn't want to be there.

"I don't take orders from you anymore, Vinny."

Mikey emerged from the backseat palming a black pistol. "Is there a problem here guys?"

Upon sight, Mox's men backed out weapons of their own and Jimmy sneakily eased toward the gas tanks.

"However you wanna do it Mikey. It's your call, but we didn't come here for that."

Vinny fumed. "Put that fuckin' thing down. I told you I'll take care of this. Now get back in the car."

"You heard your father, Mikey," Mox teased.

Mikey pressed him. "At least I know who my father is."

Mox threw a quick smirk to his team, and before Vinny could step in, the butt of his gun slammed down on Mikey's face causing him to drop his pistol. His nasal bone cracked and a stream of blood shot onto Vinny's coat.

Mox cocked the weapon and shoved it under Mikey's chin. "If your gun game was as slick as your tongue you wouldn't be in this position."

"Mox, not here!" Cleo yelled out.

"Hey!" Jimmy screamed. He was standing by one of the giant gas tanks with his .32 revolver pointed directly at it. "Either you guys put the guns down or we all die." He was trembling and the lightweight firearm felt like a 100 pound dumbbell in his hand.

Jimmy was 54 years old and had never fired a gun in his life. The only reason he kept one in the glove compartment was because he chauffeured a mob boss around the city every day and it made him feel like he was a part of that lifestyle.

"I'm tellin' you, I'll shoot this damn thing and blow half the city up. Put 'em down!"

But nobody budged.

Vinny attempted to calm him. "Easy Jimmy, I got it. Everything is cool." He grilled the five men in front of him. "What do you want Mox?"

Without removing the gun from Mikey's throat, Mox dug in his pants pocket and pulled out the photo of him, his mother and Casey. He shoved it in Vinny's face.

"My mother and father were killed in one of your buildings back in 95'. Did you know 'em?"

"Of course I knew 'em." Vinny stared at the picture. He knew the answers to all Mox's questions. "But I ain't the one you need to talk to."

Jimmy still had his gun aimed at the gas tank and Mikey was bleeding severely.

"I wanna know what you know."

Vinny side eyed Cleo. "Ask your Aunt."

"Leave my mother outta this." Cleo took a step forward.

What did his Aunt have to do with this? Mox was thrown off. He recalled asking if she knew anything about the night of the murder, but she denied it.

Mox eased off Mikey .

“Cleo, you use to be a good kid.” Vinny moved forward. “You use to listen to me. Whatever I told you to do, you did.” he leaned in close to Cleo’s face. “I liked that about you. I ate, you ate. But now... now... you and Nino Brown over here wanna take over the world together huh? Fuck Vinny and the Telesco’s. Well, you know what Cleo... when you go to sleep with the snakes, don’t be surprised when you get bit.”

“Fuck you Vinny!” Cleo snatched his weapon from the inside of his jacket and put it to Vinny’s head.”

Jimmy screamed again. “You think I’m playing!” He pulled the hammer back with his thumb and had a round ready to go.

“Hey, Cleo, I bet you never told the guys that you were the one who paid drunk Sunny to shoot up the bar and say Mox’s name.”

“You’re a fuckin’ liar Vinny.” Cleo went to smash the old man in the head with the gun, but Mox grabbed his wrist.

“We not gon’ do this here, Cleo.” Mox cut his eyes at Vinny. “This aint over.”

Vinny breathed a sigh of relief once he saw they backed away and re-entered their cars. He hadn't planned on dying today, but what he had done was plant a seed of suspicion in Mox's head. He was a wise old man if any. He knew Mox would come for him as soon as he found out the truth. All he did was buy himself some time because if Cleo and Mox were at war with each other it was beneficial to him. He needed both of them out the way so he could execute his plan.

"I knew you couldn't fuck wit' me nigga, you suck!" Tyrell tossed the PS3 controller at his homeboy Leo. He had just finished beating his ass in Madden for the third time in a row. "You see what I be doin' out there wit' that boy Ray Rice." Tyrell fixed his arm like he was a running back holding the ball and mimicked the replay that was on the screen. "Uh, uh... a lil' spin move, juke to the left. Uh! End zone nigga!"

"Shut up nigga. You better keep your voice down before Dana come back out here and kick us out. I ain't got nowhere to stay tonight my nigga."

"True... 'cause she will kick *yo'* ass out." Tyrell laughed.

He and Leo had been crashing at Dana's for the past few weeks. She agreed to let them smoke and play the game in the crib as long as they watched Brandi while she was at school.

Dana didn't have a problem helping Mox out with his daughter. She was aware of the circumstances and wanted to be of any help she could. Besides, he was funding her $40,000 a-year college tuition at Mount Sinai School of Medicine. What he didn't know was that Tyrell had been watching Brandi every night for the past month, due to the steady babysitter taking a vacation. Dana knew if he found out, he would be overly enraged, but she had no other choice. Tyrell had to watch Brandi until she found someone else.

"Roll up that dour my nigga." Tyrell tossed Leo a cigar and a zip lock bag full of weed.

Leo wiped his face with his hand and looked at the clock on the wall. "Damn son, its 5:30 already, the sun bout to come up." They had been playing the game for hours. "Aight, lemme use the bathroom first."

Two minutes later Leo came out the bathroom and sat in the fold up chair.

"You ain't flush the toilet or wash your hands?"

"Ain't no water."

"What you mean?" Tyrell hurried to the kitchen and tried the faucet.

Nothing.

"What the fuc—"

BOOM! BOOM BOOM! Open up! New Rochelle police department!!

The instant Tyrell's eyes hit the door it was flying off the hinges.

"Get on the floor! Now!" The tactical unit officer was dressed in a dark blue fatigue suit, a helmet and full bullet proof body gear, wielding a pump action, 12 gauge shotgun.

Three more officers blitzed in and searched the rest of the apartment. An hour later, Tyrell, Leo and Dana were in handcuffs sitting in holding cells at the police station and Brandi was in the custody of the state.

Dana was stunned when the detectives explained the charges and the reason for the raid. She wanted to kill her cousin.

Tyrell had been using the apartment as a trap house and his reckless behavior had cost Mox and Dana a huge loss. Police found $290,000 in cash, a 1/2 ounce of crack and a quarter pound of weed. The weed and crack was Tyrell's, but the money belonged to Mox.

As soon as the word got back to the street, Mox called a "Union" meeting.

Marriott Hotel – New Roc City

Mox walked into the 3rd floor meeting room of the Marriott in disarray. He looked defeated and fatigued, like he'd been up for days without a wink of sleep. His eyes held blood and his heart pumped misery while hellish thoughts bounced around his brain like someone pulled the lever on a pinball machine. The burden was coming down on him and the pressure was hastily getting weighted on his shoulders, but

Mox was resilient and he vowed to let nothing hinder his committal.

His dress shirt hung out one side of his pants and his shoes were untied as he neared the ash wood table. Frank, Papi and Nate were the only ones physically present because Javier would be attending via iChat and Cleo had gone missing for the last week.

Frank saw the strife on his partner's face. "Mox, don't worry we gon' take care of this."

"I hope so Frank. I feel like time might be runnin' out. Anybody heard from Cleo?" They all said no. "Frank, did you get that information I asked for?"

"Yup." He passed Mox a ripped piece of paper with a name and address on it.

Rita Davis

255 Huguenot St.

New Rochelle, NY

APT 12K

Mox tucked the piece of paper into his pocket. “Okay. We gotta make a stop by there when we finish and I gotta go check my Aunt. I also want you to go bail Dana and her little cousin out as soon as possible. I can’t have them sittin’ up in there. As far as the Telescos... we fall back for now. We don’t move until they force us to.” Mox sat on the end of the table tapping his knuckle on the wood. The strain was killing him.

Nate responded. “You sure that’s the right thing to do? You know I can make that disappear.”

“I know Nate. I just got so much shit I’m dealing with right now I can barely focus.”

Papi stood up. “Dats why we here, papi. Ju know we got ju back.”

“I think you should let Nate handle that Mox. Take some of the pressure off you. That way we can focus on getting Brandi back and handling that other thing.” Frank suggested.

Mox agreed. “You right. Nate, do that; and take Papi with you.

"Hey! You guys forget about me??" Javier broke the tension and made them all laugh. He was making his appearance through a video chat from a remote location.

Mox looked amused for the first time in hours. "Wassup, bro. How's the shoulder?"

Javier tapped on his wounded arm to show it was healing well. "Muthafucka hit me wit' a .45 Mox. I took that shit like a champ bro. I heard you took one too."

"A few pellets in the side, nothin' crazy." Mox lifted his shirt. The pellets ripped his abdomen to shreds. It looked like a sponge. "You out there takin' care of business right?"

"Of course. I should be able to set something up soon. I know you'll love it out here. Beautiful women, beautiful weather and easy money, what more could you ask for."

"I bet. Listen, Javier, stay in contact with Papi. Make sure you check in so he can keep you informed. I'ma speak to you later."

The computer screen went blank and Papi shut the laptop down.

“Before we step out this door and do what we gotta do,” Mox paused and took a good look over his team. “I jus’ wanna let each one of y’all know that I love y’all like brothers. I never had people as close to me as y’all are and I appreciate the love. This shit is genuine. We all bosses hear.” He pointed at each man and they rose from the seat they were sitting in. “No one man above the team.” Mox placed his right hand over his heart and each man followed suit. “From this day forward we pledge, under oath, to never take the stand against our fellow brothers. To never fuck each other’s wives and at all times remain loyal...” every face in the room had a cold, focused stare. “Til the heavens turn to dust and hell freezes over; let no-one stand before WE!”

SIXTEEN

Susan leaned against the bathroom sink and let the salty droplets fall from her eye wells to the porcelain tiles. She wiped her face for the hundredth time and tried to catch her breath. “Please stop!” she cried. With each bang on the door, her nerves would flinch. She was frightened and exhausted from putting up the fight of her life and barely getting away. The last sixty minutes she had been living out the most terrifying dream you could imagine and now she was locked in her own bathroom, praying that someone would come and save her.

“Bitch, as soon as you open this door I’ma fuckin’ kill you.” Cleo had his back against the bathroom door. He clenched a half gallon of Hennessy in his right hand and a 5 inch, sandal wood handle kitchen knife in the other. He was pissy drunk and his disposition was unstable. “Su-san!” he slurred and then turned the cognac bottle up to his lips. He lifted his right leg and horse kicked the bathroom door with his size 13 Timberland.

"Cleo, please stop! Why are you doing this to me?" Susan wiped her runny nose and tried to get her hands to stop shaking.

Cleo kicked again, but this time his foot crashed through the flimsy plywood door. He kicked some more to widen the hole and then he got down on the floor and stuck his head through the crack like Jack Nicholson in the *Shining*.

"Heeeeere's Johnny!" He laughed so hard he started to cough. "Susan!" he screamed. After several unsuccessful attempts to reach the lock, Cleo finally got smart and used the knife to move the latch.

Susan had nowhere to turn, nowhere to run and nowhere to hide. She had to fight. She thought back on her previous abusive relationships and all the beatings she took from the men who claimed they loved her. *Was this love?* She felt like the only men she attracted were the ones that used physical force. It was a cycle. She watched her father violate her mother time and time again, so much to the point that it became normal and if it didn't happen, then something was wrong.

She balled her fist so hard, her finger nails cut into her palm and she charged at Cleo as he came through the door. The Hennessy bottle slipped from his fingers and hit the floor. Shards of glass and cognac were everywhere.

Susan took a chance and tried to reach for the knife in his hand, but slipped on the wet, glassy tile and banged her head on the enamel steel bathtub. The impact knocked her unconscious instantly and she lay there, on her own bathroom floor, powerless and damn near dead.

Cleo dropped the knife in the toilet and got down on the floor beside her. He was still in a drunken stupor. “Susan.” he shook her limp body, but she didn’t respond. He lifted her and held her in his arms. “Baby, get up.” he used the back of his hand to wipe the blood that leaked down the side of her mouth; the blood that he drew just an hour ago after he slapped her. “Baby,” he mumbled. “Get up.”

Susan was still alive but her breaths were quick, short and faint and if she didn’t receive medical attention soon, she would die.

“I’m sorry, baby...” Tears washed Cleo’s face. He rocked her in his arms. “I’m sorry...”

His cell phone vibrated in his pocket and snapped him out his drunkenness for a second. He dug it out and saw it was Mox calling. He quickly hit accept.

“Mox, I need your help.” He looked down at Susan. She hadn’t moved yet.

Mox could hear the conflict in his voice. It sounded like he was crying. “Cleo, what happened? Where you at?”

Cleo closed his eyes. “Mox, I’m sorry…” his voice got high.

“Cleo!” Where are you?”

“I’m at Susan’s.” He sniffled. “Mox hurry up, please.”

“Where’s she at?”

He whispered into the speaker. “She’s sleepin’”

“Aight, I’ll be there, don’t move.”

25 Minutes Later

"Cleo!" Mox yelled as he pushed the door open to the brownstone. "Frank, call his cell phone back." he removed the .40 caliber black Taurus from the double harness shoulder holster underneath his blazer.

"He's not answering Mox."

The two of them cautiously ascended the steps to the second level and Mox hollered again. "Cleo, you in here!?"

They heard some shuffling towards the back of the house.

He could hardly get the words out. "Yeah... I'm...I'm in the bathroom."

When Mox and frank turned the corner, the bathroom door was wide open with a gaping hole in it like someone kicked through it. Cleo was on the floor holding Susan, who looked to be either sleep or dead.

"What the fuck?" Mox tucked his gun back in the holster and ran over to the bathroom. "Yo Frank, check the house and make sure nobody else is here." he looked down at Cleo's bloody hands and Susan's beat up face. "What the fuck did you do, Cleo?"

"Mox, I'm sorry..." His face was full of tears and Susan's blood.

Mox snatched a towel off the rack and threw it on the floor, so he wouldn't slip in the glass. He bent down and put two fingers under Susan's chin and felt for a pulse.

"She's still breathing. We gotta hurry up and get her to a hospital. Cleo, get up!"

Mox and Frank carried Susan out to the car and put her in the back seat with Cleo. Frank got behind the wheel and they rushed through the moderate traffic. They made a right onto Amsterdam and then a left onto 135th street and ran almost every light until they reached the Harlem Hospital Center.

Mox pulled Susan from the car and waved down the ambulance that pulled up to the emergency entrance. The two EMTs got Susan onto a gurney and into the emergency room without delay. Mox couldn't stay and give any information, so he hopped back in the car and they took off.

After a ten minute ride on the highway going back uptown, Mox told Frank to pull into a White Castle's parking lot on Westchester Avenue. He jumped out, pulled the back door open and Frank tried to stop him. "Mox, leave him alone."

“What the fuck is wrong wit’ you, Cleo!? What you do to that girl?” Mox dragged his 300 pound frame out the backseat like a bag of laundry.

Cleo didn’t even put up a struggle. He just cried. “Mox, I’m sorry...”

“Yo, Mox, it’s a lot of police out here tonight. I think we need to keep it movin’.” Frank was trying to avoid any more problems because they already had enough to deal with.

After Cleo got back in the car they continued on the highway to New Rochelle.

“Frank, drop me off on Huguenot so I can go see Ms. Davis.”

“Got you.”

“And keep this nigga wit’ you. Don’t let him out your sight.”

Vito downed his last shot of Johnny Walker and got off the bar stool he was sitting on. He checked his watch, smiled and thought about his late night rendezvous that would take place within the next hour. He hadn't gotten laid in almost a month. Better yet, more than a month.

Tony slid down the bar with a washrag, wiping up spilled drinks and peanut shells. He stopped when he reached Vito. "Boss, you taking it in early tonight?"

"Yeah, I got a hot one, Tony." He fixed his sweater and tapped his pocket to make sure he still had cash on him. "Twin blondes," he cheesed.

"A regular stud ain't you..." Tony laughed. He just knew Vito was telling one of his routine lies. But not tonight, for the first time, he was actually telling the truth.

"Go head and makes jokes, Tony... 'cause in about twenty minutes I'll be bangin' two 20 year olds from the back on a bum knee. You'll be at home... by yourself of course, drinking stale beer and slammin' lil' Sammy there in your pants. Ha! Now make sure you lock up on time," Vito turned to exit. "And don't rip the skin off your dick tonight, Tony. Take it easy!"

"Fuck you Vito!" Tony threw the washrag and almost hit him in the back.

Jimmy had been sitting in the limo, parked in front of Vito's for the last twenty minutes waiting on him to come out.

Vito jumped in the backseat and tapped on the partition. "Jimmy, take me over to the Ritz Carlton, Three Renaissance Square."

The limo peeled off and he sat back stargazing on the adventure he planned on having with the twins. He envisioned all the different positions he would have them in and the thought alone aroused him. He needed to get ready.

He reached into his pocket and pulled out a folded hundred dollar bill. He opened it up and dumped the white, powder like crystals onto the back of his hand and then he vacuumed it right up his nostrils. The rush was immediately electric and numbing and the feeling was euphoric.

He sat composed and let the high potency drug run its course through his blood stream as he relaxed in paradise. When he finally looked out the window to see where he was, they were just passing the Ritz Carlton.

"Jimmy, where the fuck you goin'? You passed the place."

He kept it steady down Court St. and made a left onto East Post Road and then pulled over and parked behind a black van.

“Jimmy, didn’t you fuckin’ hear me. I sai—”

The partition came all the way down. “I no think Jimmy hear you, my friend.” Papi lifted Jimmy’s stiff body from out the passenger seat and Vito saw the dime sized bullet hole that sat in the center of his forehead with a streak of blood flowing down the bridge of his nose. “I no think Jimmy hear nobody, my friend.”

Vito fumbled, trying to grab the pistol off his waistline, but when the door came open he fell into a state of shock. Like a deer caught in bright headlights, he couldn’t move.

Nate was standing in a black suit, gripping an AM-15 sub machine gun. “Too late Vito.” He let the machine gun blow, and fire shot from the nozzle like a torch. The sub sounded like a jackhammer going off in the middle of the night and Vito caught every bullet that came out of it. He fell to the limo carpet and half of his body was hanging out the door. His blood was splattered throughout the back of the car.

Nate looked down at Vito’s bloody corpse and kicked him over to make sure he wasn’t breathing. “Papi, vamanos!”

Papi emerged from the driver's seat, tossed Jimmy's hat and jacket back in the car and him and Nate got in the black van that was parked ten feet away and burnt the road up.

Mox stepped out the black 500 Benz and walked into the Avalon apartments at 255 Huguenot Street. He gave the desk attendant a fake name and told him he was visiting someone one the ninth floor, but he took the elevator to twelve. He tapped on the door that had 12K on it and waited for someone to answer.

An elderly female voice came from behind the door. "Who is it?"

"Hello, Mrs. Davis... It's Mox. I'm Priscilla's friend."

The lock clicked and the door slowly came open. The older woman standing before him had a familiar face, one that he recognized. Mrs. Davis had a few more wrinkles, but for the most part she and Priscilla looked just alike. They were both beautiful and even in her old age, she carried a delightful semblance.

“Look at those eyes.” She shook her head. “Come in, Mox. I was wondering when you would stop by.”

He stepped in and gave Mrs. Davis a kiss on the cheek and then followed her into the living room.

The apartment was a modest one; bare, eggshell colored walls, a micro fiber couch and loveseat, a 32 inch flat screen television sitting on a stand against the far wall and tall plants in each corner of the room.

Mrs. Davis went into the kitchen and poured Mox and herself some water. She sat the two glasses on the table along with a white envelope that had his name on it and took a seat on the couch. Mox rested in the loveseat next to her.

“Well, it’s a pleasure meeting you Mox. I haven’t heard too much about you, but I do know that my daughter loves you.” She smiled and sipped her water. “You see that picture over there?” she pointed to a photo on the T.V stand. It was a picture of him and Priscilla the day Mox brought his 430 CLK. They were leaning against the car, parked in front of the dealership. “Whenever Priscilla walks through that door, the first thing she does is pick that picture up and dust the frame. She loves her some Mox.”

He got up to look at the picture. He had only seen it one time before this. "I love her too Mrs. Davis. That's why I'm here." Mox picked the picture up and stared at it. A recollection of that day materialized in his brain. It felt like it had just happened.

He saw how happy Priscilla was and then he thought on how wearied she had looked the last time he'd seen her. He wanted to cry. He wanted to fall out and snivel right there in the middle of Mrs. Davis' living room. His heart was sore and contorted because he believed his self-centeredness may have been the cause of her stress, and down the line she didn't make rational decisions.

"Have you heard from her?" He asked.

"In the last year, I got two letters from Priscilla. One was mines..." She pushed the envelope on the table closer to Mox. "And this one is yours."

He picked it up and ripped it open:

Mox,

I not writing this letter to apologize for anything I did in the past. If I did it, it was meant to be done. You left me when things got rough and I tried. I tried my hardest to hate every bone in your body, but I couldn't. It's just something that's not allowing me to have any type of animosity towards you and I can't even explain it.

When I found out I was pregnant with Brandi I was overjoyed. I wanted the chance to speak to you so bad, so that I could tell you we were going to have a child, but that never happened.

For six long years I wondered what was going on with you. I didn't know if you were dead, sick or what. I was lost without you, Mox and it never even crossed your mind that someone on the outside, who truly loved you, was concerned.

Leaving all that in the past; today is a new day and I now have a clear and precise outlook on my life. I've been in this rehabilitation center for the past few months and things are going pretty good. I'm looking forward to coming home and seeing Brandi. How's she doing?

Mox, if it's not too much to ask, my mother's rent is two months past due and I'm not able to take care of her the way I was when I was there. We don't get along, but I did make sure she had a roof over her head and food in her refrigerator. Whatever you can part with will be appreciated.

I should be coming home any day now. The counselors in this program are helping me find an apartment, get a job and enroll back into school. I'm excited. I can't wait to start over and I also can't wait to see my babygirl.

Things are different now Mox. Maybe there's still room for US.

Love you! And see you soon!!

Priscilla,

P.S. Tell my baby I love her and give her a HUGE kiss for me.

Mox put the letter back in the envelope and sat down. "Mrs. Davis, I got something I need to speak to you about." He wasn't prepared to tell her, but he had to. He was thinking maybe she could help the process go a little smoother. He breathed deep. "I don't know if Priscilla told you, but she left Brandi with me and there's a little problem now."

"What do you mean?"

Mox got straight to the point. "I had someone babysit Brandi while I was working and this particular person's house got raided by the police. They found drugs and money in the apartment and CPS took Brandi."

"Oh, my God... Mox you have to get her back. Priscilla will go crazy. Oh, poor baby. I know my little angel is scared."

"I know. That's part of the reason for me coming here. I need your help."

Mrs. Davis stood up. "If it has anything to do with Priscilla or Brandi, I'm sorry but I can't get involved."

Mox was stunned. *How could she say something like that? This was her blood.* "I don't understand. This is your granddaughter I'm talking about. I would go get her if I could, but my name isn't on her birth certificate. It has to be immediate family. If you go in there, there's no way they can deny you. We can go get her today."

The distressed expression on her face wasn't the one Mox was looking for. "I'm sorry Mox, I can't. A long time ago Priscilla told me to stay out of her and Brandi's life... and that's how it's been since that day. It hurts, don't get me wrong. I love my daughter and my grandchild, but that's a road that I refuse to travel down again. Priscilla may not have told you how tainted our relationship is and I'm not going to get into it because if she wants you to know, she'll tell you, but what I will say is, we've never had a good standing between us and that's just what it is. I wish it was different, but it's not."

He tried to understand, but he just couldn't. "So, you're not gonna help me?"

"Mox, the only thing I can do for you is pray and have faith in God because he always does the right thing. Sometimes we may ask why and other times we even doubt him, but trust me, if you have credence and you admit Him into your life He will heal you and guide you down that path of rectitude and spiritual bliss... and then you can begin to understand why things happen the way they do."

Religion was something Mox never really delved into, although during his incarceration he did thumb through the Bible a couple of times and study a few scriptures out of the Quran, but he wasn't too apprehensive on acquiring the knowledge of a single creed. His sharpest memory of God had been the prayer he heard before he saw his mother and father's ravaged bodies.

If we confess our sins, he is faithful and just and will forgive us our sins and purify us from all unrighteousness.

He had memorized the prayer from that moment on. To him it meant if he admitted his wrong doings to God he wouldn't be judged, but forgiven and cleansed of sin.
Mox got up to leave. There was nothing more he could say. He gave Mrs. Davis a hug and a peck on the cheek. "I have no choice but to respect your decision. I wish things were different between you and your daughter, but I see that's something you and her have to handle." He reached into his pocket and pulled out a stack of one hundred dollar bills and a piece of paper with his name and number on it. He counted out two thousand dollars and put the money and his information on the table. "If you ever have a change of heart, I'm only a phone call away. The money is for groceries and anything else you need. I'll make sure the

rent is paid until Priscilla comes back so you don't have to worry about that.

"Mox, thank you, but I can't take your money."

He smiled and opened the door. "You got no choice."

SEVENTEEN

The teeming rains cascaded from the dusky, grey clouds that loomed in the air on the pained Friday morning of Vito Telesco's funeral. It was a spectacle. The bosses from all five families were in attendance including a number of immediate family members and friends who were there to show support to each other in a time of grief.

Vinny's wife, daughter and son stood alongside him under large, black umbrellas, shedding tears and watching as they lowered the $12,000 gold trimmed casket into the ground. Vito's final resting place would be the St. John's cemetery in Middle Village Queens, NY where a private mausoleum held the body of one of the most infamous crime figures in history, Salvatore (Charlie) "Lucky" Luciano.

Domenic Conte, the boss of the Gambino family walked over to Vinny before everyone left the cemetery. He was wearing a long, oyster colored trench coat, shiny black shoes and a matching fedora. He grabbed Vinny's hand and kissed both sides of his face. "Mi dispiace (I'm sorry) Vinny, little Vito was like a son to me. I remember when he was born, God bless him. Hey," he moved in closer to whisper in Vinny's ear. "Hurry up and take care of this fuckin' thing before it gets outta hand. I don't wanna get involved." He patted Vinny on the back and went to get in his car.

Mikey saw the strain all over his father's face. "Pop, you okay?"

"I just had to bury your brother, Mikey. What do you think?" Vinny opened the limousine door and got into the back seat.

"Well, if you need me to do anything just let me know."

The back window came down and Vinny scowled. "I want their fuckin' heads Mikey, all of 'em... Mox, Cleo, the mother, brothers, sisters, cousins... whoever got the same blood running through their veins is fuckin' dead!" he spat. "You better handle this Mikey and I'm not joking around."

The window went up and the limousine rolled away.

EIGHTEEN

The Charles K. Post Treatment & Rehabilitation Center in Brentwood, Long Island is where Priscilla had spent her last 120 days. After Ryan humiliated her in the street, she kept her promise and signed into the program in order to make a change for the betterment of her and Brandi's life. She was fully aware that at the pace she had been running the streets, it wouldn't have been too much longer before she would have gotten locked up and or even worse, killed.

The time away allowed her to reflect on the series of events that led up to her decline. Since the day Mox disappeared out of her life, everything began to go downhill. She couldn't digest the fact that one day he was there and they were together, connected like links in a chain and then, he was gone and she was abandoned. Things really got bad when Priscilla found out she was pregnant with Brandi. That's when she fell into an unmanageable state of depression and with Ryan feeding her drugs; it only worsened her state of mind.

It took a few weeks for it to register, but after a while, Priscilla realized that Mox wasn't coming back anytime soon. She was still getting coke from Juan Carlos, but when she got with Ryan he couldn't move the same amount of weight as Mox had been moving and the money was coming up short every time.

After taking too many losses, Juan Carlos told Priscilla he was no longer doing business with her until Mox returned.

Now she was pregnant, broke, and had recently developed a new drug habit that she couldn't afford. The only thing left to do was exactly what she had vowed to never do and that was become what her mother had always called her.

Ryan had never given Priscilla a dime, so when she went broke; she had to do for herself. Whatever it took to put food and clean diapers on her baby girl, she did. Plenty of nights, she would starve because the only money she could hustle up would be enough for some formula for Brandi. She stole everything from bottles of Gerber baby food out of Stop & Shop to an $800 dollar power folding stroller out of Toys R Us.

She ran a scam on the department of social services and figured out a way to get much more money than she should have been getting. The extra finances helped her secure her own living space. She was able to rent a room for $500 a month.

Every day, Priscilla would tell herself that she was going to kick the habit, but every day the habit continued to kick her. By the time Brandi was 4 years old, Priscilla was all the way strung out on cocaine and the effects of the highly addictive drug were more than obvious. Certain areas of her skin darkened and her hair became dry and frizzled. The only thing she thought about throughout the day was coke. It got so bad that her sinus and nostril tissue were permanently scarred. She no longer loved herself inside or out. She didn't care. She became physically dependent on the drug and needed it to function.

But everything changed the moment she walked through the doors of the treatment center. It felt like a ton of weight fell from her shoulders as soon as she signed the agreement papers.

The first week of her withdrawal was the worst because her body craved more of the drug than usual and her obsession to use had increased. Instead of giving in to her cravings,

Priscilla had to occupy her mind with new and unconnected thoughts to distance herself from the norm. She had to become somebody new, and in order to do that she needed to let it all out.

When she started her one on one therapy sessions with her counselor, Priscilla was distant and unresponsive. She wasn't comfortable opening up to people she knew, so a stranger was out of the question. It took some time, but eventually she started to express herself and show some progress.

A couple weeks later she was ready for the group sessions.

"Hello, my name is Priscilla... and I'm an addict."

On her journey through the 12 step program, Priscilla discovered a new life and gradually shed all the fear and emotions she kept locked inside of her. It was a new breath and a rejuvenated experience. She listened as other addicts shared their stories of joy and horror and when it became her turn, she was delighted to partake.

"Hello, my name is Priscilla and I'm addicted to cocaine."

"Hello, Priscilla." The group said together.

She continued. “I came here four months ago after my ex-boyfriend beat me up in the streets. I’m thirty years old and I have a six year old daughter who I abandoned just so I could go off and get high. Excuse me y’all.” her eyes got watery and she wiped them.

“It’s alright, baby...” A white girl named Jennifer said. She and Priscilla had had met through the program three months ago. They had been cool since. “We all made mistakes that we knew were wrong when we were doing them. It’s all good. Jus’ let it out.”

Jennifer was the only friend Priscilla had in the program. Everybody gravitated to at least one person they could trust and confide in and she was just that. She and Priscilla had a lot in common. They were beautiful, young females with daughters, a drug habit and tons of hate in their blood towards their mothers.

Priscilla kept going. “I never told anyone this, but when I was nine years old my mother and father were separated and not too long after she had a new boyfriend. From the day he walked through the door I knew he was the devil. I tried to tell my mother how I felt and she just brushed my feelings off to the side. After six months of them dating she let this stranger move into our house. There were nights I would jump out of my sleep because I felt someone's presence and sure enough, it would be him, standing over me, drilling me with those satanic like eyes of his."

Her tears started to flow again, but this time she let them fall. "It started with the disgusting looks and it escalated to him touching me and eventually he pinned me down in my own bed and raped me." The entire room had an eerie silence and nobody could look Priscilla in the face. "I told my mother about it the next day and you know what she did?" Priscilla paused. "That bitch told me I was lying and she whopped my ass everyday faithfully, until I told her I had made the story up. Till this day she still doesn't believe he raped me."

Her story had the whole room in tears. Jennifer got up from her seat and went over to give Priscilla a hug. They cried and embraced for a minute. Priscilla had just rid herself of dead weight she had been holding onto for twenty years and it felt remarkable. It helped her move on to the next phase of her new life.

All 18 group members stood up and started clapping. They were proud of the progress Priscilla had made since her arrival and in a few hours she would be on her way out the door to start her new life.

Jennifer tapped her leg. “Hey, you better not forget about me when you get back in the world.”

Priscilla hugged her again. “You know I got you girl. I told you I got a plan...”

NINETEEN

The fairly sized one bedroom apartment smelled of soiled clothes that hadn't been washed in months. The walls were filled with smoke and the carpet was full of dirt. Tyrell sat on the arm of the old ripped up sofa and reached into his left pocket. He pulled out 2 quarters, a dime and 5 nickels.

Eighty five fuckin' cent to my name. He thought.

"Tyrell!"

"What do you want, Ma?"

"Gimme some money."

He looked down at the change in his hand and smiled, but he really wanted to cry. "I ain't got no money."

"So gimme some drugs then." Ms. Michaels staggered out the back and into the living room. She was a tall, slim woman, who once was exceptionally attractive, but after smoking crack for 5 years, that beauty quickly dwindled away. She had a grubby red scarf tied around her head to hide her bald spots and her T-shirt and sweatpants were unwashed and full of holes.

"I ain't got nothin' ma. No money, no drugs." He pushed some old newspapers to the side and sat on the sofa.

She scratched at a dark spot on her neck. "Well you gotta get the fuck outta here. I don't need you here if you ain't got nothin'… you might as well go back to where you was."

"I was at cousin Dana's house, but she said I couldn't stay there no more. I ain't got nowhere to go."

"Well you going outta here… bet that."

"Ma, don't do this to me right now. Please."

"Please my ass, Tyrell. You wanna be grown, take yo' grown ass out there in them streets.

Tyrell cast a hateful sneer at his mother. "Oh, so since I ain't got no money or no drugs I gotta *leave*? You gon' kick your own son out over some foul shit like *that*?"

Ms. Michaels picked up a half smoked cigarette out the ashtray and lit it. “Boy please...”

“Fuck you then... you crack head bitch!” He slammed the door as he left out.

“No, fuck you, Tye-rell! You no-good-son-of-a-bitch!” She ranted. “You aint shit and you never gon’ be shit! You just like yo’ ol’ punk ass father!”

It wasn’t the first time Tyrell had called her a crack head or a bitch. Their altercations started the day he found out she was using. His heart felt like it had gotten crushed and on top of that, he got ridiculed for it. That’s when the trouble started.

Two years ago, he solidified his hood credibility when he shot and robbed two dudes from out of town at a dice game in the hood.

“Yo, that’s in the crack!”

“Everything good over here. I told you the rules before we started.”

Tyrell stood off to the side watching the local hustlers spar it off with the dice like he did every night in the hood.

Stacks of money, liquor, weed and women always set the scene for a summer night in the hood and the gamblers stayed out all night. Some nights, C-low games would go on for hours and then lead into the next day.

After about five straight hours the only ones still going at it were Rome and two dudes from out of town.

"I'm not payin' that. It's in the crack. Let me roll over." The short kid from out of town said.

Rome stuffed the dice in his pocket. "You not gon' pay me? Nigga that's a five hunit dolla ace. You gon' pay that."

The tall kid from out of town said, "My man said let him roll over."

Rome gave Tyrell the head nod and he got off the bench. "Fuck you and your man. Gimme all that shit!" he pulled out an old .38 snub nose with black electrical tape wrapped around the handle.

"Yo, Rome wassup wit cha—"

"Shut the fuck up!" Tyrell slapped the tall kid from out of town with the old pistol and then went in his pockets and took everything he had. He did the same to the short kid, but when he went to take the chain off his neck, the short kid got bold and tried to grab the gun. He didn't succeed. Tyrell shot them both right there in front of the building and from that day on, the hood would respect him as a certified G.

After his mother told him he wasn't shit, Tyrell went and rolled his last bag of weed and sat in the park smoking and thinking of a come up. He was out on bail, no money, no work and no place to lay his head. The only thing he owned was that old, rusted .38 snub nose with the tape on the handle. He had to make do with what he had.

Halfway through the blunt, his homie Leo popped up. "Whaddup, Rell?" he took a seat on the wooden bench.

"Coolin, what's good wit' you? Wanna hit this?" he tried to pass the blunt, but Leo said no. "Oh, you quit smoking now, huh?"

"Yeah, I'm chillin'. I gotta get my shit together, Rell. I can't keep doin' the same shit. Yo, my moms said she gon' kick me out if I get in any more trouble. Fuck I'ma go?"

"Nigga, my moms already kicked me out. You know how that goes... fuck it." Tyrell inhaled a thick stream of smoke and exhaled through his nostrils. "What you got in the bag?"

"DVD's and socks." Leo opened the bag and took the contents out.

Tyrell laughed loud and the smoke caused him to cough. His eyes were watery. "Nigga, you sellin' DVD's and socks now, what the fuck is wrong wit' you?"

"I ain't tryna go to jail, that's what's wrong wit' me. Fuck that crack shit. My uncle fronted me some stock and this shit is good money. Police ain't gon' fuck wit' me for this shit."

Tyrell just shook his head. "Nigga you trippin'... yo, come wit' me to go see Rome real quick. He 'pose to give me some bread." They got up and walked into building 70. Tyrell was still joking on Leo's hustle. "You a funny nigga, son. What door this nigga live at?"

"I think it's 2C." Leo answered. They walked up the steps and Tyrell knocked on the door.

A male voice shouted. "Who is it?"

"It's Rell."

The door came open. "What you want lil' nigga?" Rome said. He kept the door cracked with his foot behind it.

“Yo, lemme holla at you for a sec my nigga.”

Rome opened the door and let Tyrell and Leo in. “Damn, this shit is nice Rome.”

Tyrell looked over the nicely situated apartment. Rome had been doing fairly well for himself these past few years. He was one of a handful of hustlers in the projects who were really getting some money. He ran a profitable dope spot on the other side of town that had been in business for the last three years and sometimes he would get Tyrell to do a few things for him. Rome recognized the thirst in his eyes and took advantage of young Tyrell because he was easily swayed. He fed him just enough to keep him hungry and coming back for more, but Tyrell wasn’t as stupid as he thought.

Rome knew he came to ask for something. “So wassup, what you wanna talk about?”

“I need to hold somethin’?”

“You always need to hold somethin’ my nigga. Every time I give you somethin’ you fuck it up.”

Tyrell tried to reason. “I’m sayin’ my nigga... I know I fucked shit up before, but right now shit is real. I ain’t got nowhere to rest my head. I ain't got no bread. I need your help, for real."

Rome wasn't giving in this time. "I ain't fuckin' wit' you like that Rell. It's too much of a headache." he looked at Leo. "What the fuck you lookin' at? What you got in the bag, Leo?"

"DVD's and socks."

Rome looked in the bag. "Oh, word... lemme get a couple pair of them joints and that new shit that came out Friday... wit' Denzel." Leo gave him the DVD and two pairs of socks. "Okay, I see you Leo. You gettin' money huh? So, this is what you need that paper for Tyrell?"

"Man... fuck them DVD's Rome. I need some real money."

"Nigga you tryna be Pablo Escobar *tomorrow*. That shit ain't gon' happen. You gotta start at the bottom and put that work in. You know the old saying, *'Rome wasn't built in a day'* " he laughed. "Hold up y'all... I gotta go check on my daughter. She's in the back sleep." He walked to the backroom.

"Yo," Leo whispered when he saw Tyrell snatch the pistol from his pants. "What the fuck you doing?"

Tyrell palmed the weapon, looked at it and then eyed Leo. “Jus’ shut up and do what I tell you to,” he said.

“But—”

Rome came from out the back and as soon as he entered the living room, he saw Tyrell holding the gun. “What you doin’?” his eyes were on the old taped up gun. “Fuck you got that for?”

Tyrell was nervous. He quickly aimed the gun at Rome’s head. “Where the fuckin’ money at Rome?”

Rome grinned. He didn’t think Tyrell was serious. He looked at Leo and noticed the panic on his face, so he took a step toward the gun. “Stop playin’ wit’ me Rell.”

Tyrell took a step forward and gripped the handgun tighter. He wasn’t playing at all. “You think it’s a joke?” He pulled the trigger and shot Rome in the foot.

Leo jumped at the sound of the gunshot. “Rell what the fuck are you doing!?”

The impact from the bullet broke Rome’s ankle and he fell to the floor in agony. The look he gave Tyrell was a confused one. "You buggin lil' nigga... chill!" Blood was spilling out the hole in his foot.

Tyrell stood over him and put the gun to his head. "Where that bread at nigga?"

Leo was scared to death. "Rome, I aint have nothin' to do wit' this," he pleaded.

"Shut the fuck up, Leo before I shoot your dumb ass too." He bought his eyes back to Rome. "You got five seconds to tell me where that money at. Five..." he started counting down.

"Rell don't do this, my daughter is in the back. Please."

"Three... Two..."

Rome had to make a swift decision. "Aight... aight." he took a deep breath and looked at all the blood coming from his foot. "The money is in the deep freezer, all the way at the bottom." The pain was worsening. "Ta... take it and get the fuck outta here."

"Leo... get that." Tyrell ordered.

His adrenalin was at its peak. Every time held that gun in his hand he felt powerful. The power was so intense it stimulated his mind and made him believe that he was everything he ever wanted to be. It was magician like and the gun was his magic wand. He could make things happen with just a wave of his hand.

A loud baby's cry echoed from the back room and right away Rome's neck turned. It was his 3 year old baby girl, Essence. She had been asleep the whole time.

“C'mon Rell, let me get my daughter, man.” Rome tried to stand up, but his body weight was too much pressure for his wounded limb. He slouched back down to the floor. He attempted to crawl to the back room, but Tyrell stopped him with a harsh, soccer player kick to the ribs and Rome curled into a fetal position on the cold tile.

Leo came from out the kitchen holding two giant zip-lock freezer bags filled with money. He was sweating and agitated with terror. “Rome,” he whined, shaking his head. “I didn't have nothin' to do wit' this.”

Tyrell turned the pistol on Leo. “Shut yo' stupid ass up and wait by the door,” he tossed him a shopping bag. “Put the money in that bag.”

The baby's cries grew louder by the passing minutes and Rome continued to lose blood. “Yo, Rell you got everything, man…" he cried. "Jus' go… please let me get to my daughter."

Tyrell glanced down at the blood on the floor and then looked at Rome begging for his life. There was no way he could leave this apartment without killing him. He knew if he let Rome live, as soon as he was able to walk, he would come gunning for him. He raised the revolver and leveled it to Rome's head. He bit down on his bottom lip until he split it and tasted his own blood. He was so focused he didn't hear Leo's cries for him to not shoot.

"Please, don't shoot him," he begged.

Tyrell strangled the pistol's hair trigger and unloaded a slug into Rome's head and then he pumped the last three in his chest. Besides the gunshots, all you heard was Essence in the back room screaming her baby lungs out.

Leo fumbled trying to unlock the door. His nerves were rattled. When he finally got it open, he took off running toward the staircase and Tyrell was right behind him.

"Hold up…" Tyrell yanked the back of Leo's shirt preventing him from continuing down the steps. "Let's go up to the roof and go over." When Leo turned around, his face was wet from tears. "What the fuck you cryin' for nigga?"

"You didn't have to kill 'em Rell." Leo bawled. The teardrops were flowing freely.

Tyrell took the bag of money from him and snatched him up by the back of his shirt. "Get the fuck up the steps nigga."

They hurried up the stairs to the roof of building 70 and crossed over to building 81. They were the only two connecting buildings in the projects. Before they reached the lobby in 81, Tyrell pushed Leo against the wall in the staircase and pressed the snub nosed barrel to his cheek. "If you say a word about what happened to *anybody*... I'ma kill you. You hear me?" Leo nodded. "Go to the crib, act like nothing happened and I'ma come see you tomorrow wit' some money."

Leo could care less about the money; he was pleased with walking away with his life. Him and Tyrell spilt up and went their separate ways.

TWENTY

July 1st 2011

The sun was beating down on the project bricks at a sweltering 98 degrees when Mox hopped out the United taxi cab and tried to rush into his Aunt's building. Halfway there he got stopped by his Uncle Wise Earl. "Playboy...you goin' upstairs, I need to holla you at real quick." Uncle Wise was getting old, but he was still as sharp as a scorpion's stinger and his smooth 70's style had yet to be modified. He was an ol' school player who played by the ol' school rules.

Earl had come up in the era of the *"Real Gangsters"* where if somebody was caught stealing, depending on the value, either your hand would be chopped off at the wrist or a few fingers would go missing. It was the time when guys in the streets had morals and principals. If something got done it was with a reason behind it and not *"just because"*

Although this new generation didn't abide by these rules anymore; Uncle Earl did.

"Wassup, Unc... how you been?" Mox could see he had fresh track marks from shooting heroin into his veins. Earl had kicked the habit for a few years, but the monkey was back for revenge.

He followed his nephew into his sister's building. "Maintainin'... tyrna dodge these goddamn suckers as usual. Hey, you heard about that boy Rome?"

"Nah, what happened to him?"

"Young boy put somethin' hot in 'em. They found him in his apartment shot up last night. Police came and snatched up that young nigga, Leo."

"Get the fuck outta here, are you serious?" Mox had just bailed Dana, Tyrell and Leo out of the county jail. "You fuckin' around again, Unc?"

Earl glanced down at the marks on his arms. "Listen, nephew. You let me worry about this bitch on my back and let's continue to take care of that business. You hear me?"

They stepped off the elevator and Mox put the key in the door. “You full of shit, Unc. How you expect to conduct business and you noddin’ off n’ shit?”

Earl frowned. He disliked when people told him the truth about his addiction. “Aight, keep your voice down, Sybil don’t know I’m getting’ high.” he closed the door behind him.

“Oh, word?...” Mox peeked his head in the kitchen looking for his aunt. “Auntie!” he shouted.

“Yes?” Sybil came from out the back and saw Earl and Mox standing in the living room. “What you want Mox, I’m watchin’ my stories.”

“Your brother is back out there getting’ high.”

Earl was shocked. He couldn’t believe Mox would do him like that.

Sybil looked at her brother’s face and then at his arms and when he tried to hide the scars, she knew Mox was telling the truth. “I don’t know why the fuck you tryna hide ‘em for Earl. Anybody with eyes can see that shit is in you. I was just too naïve. I got blinded and so caught up on believing in you and knowing you could make that change that I forgot who I was dealing with. You know how that saying goes, *'once a junkie always a junkie.'*."

Earl got defensive. "I know I fucked up, but don't act like you this goddamn angel who fell from heaven and you ain't never did wrong. We all done did some shit we regret. Fuck it." Earl threw his hands in the air. "Since my shit is all out on the table, we might as well put *everything* on the muthafuckin table!"

"You right, Unc. We gon' put everything on the table today. I got some questions and I need 'em answered." Mox glanced at his aunt. He saw the discomfiture in the shift of her demeanor. "When's the last time you spoke to Cleo, auntie?"

Sybil walked into the kitchen. "I was just on the phone with him. He's across town."

"Call him back." As soon as the words came out of Mox's mouth the front door was coming open and Cleo was walking through it. Mox hadn't seen him since two nights prior when they had to rush Susan to the emergency room. "Cleo... wassup, you right on time," he smiled.

"On time for what?" he was confused.

Mox wasted no time. “Auntie, I know you been holding secrets from me about the night of my parents murder. I’m not leaving this living room until you tell me the truth.”

“Mox, I don’t have to tell you anything.”

Earl cut in. “Yes you do, because if you don’t, I will.”

“What the fuck are y’all talkin’ about?” Cleo was still lost.

Sybil stayed silent and kept her eyes glued to Earl.

“Cat got your tongue, sis? Let me help you out...” Earl turned to Mox. “That nigga Reginald ain’t your real father, we been lying to you your whole life. Your—”

Sybil pulled a picture out the Bible that was sitting on the coffee table and passed it to Mox. “That’s your real father.”

Mox looked down at the picture and his body froze up. He couldn’t believe the person he was staring at was his biological father, but he knew it had to be true because his eyes told him so.

Sybil tried to explain. “Me and your mother used to go out a lot. They knew us at damn near every club in the city when we were younger. Both of us were gorgeous, but your mother had that *‘talk’* she could convince a nigga to do anything she asked for just by having a formal conversation. Dudes went crazy for my sister. The day I met him" she pointed to the picture. "Me and your mother was in some club and he approached me. Wanda kept telling me to go talk to him and eventually I did. That night we had all been drinking and smoking so everyone was intoxicated and I did something I probably wouldn't have done had I not been drinking. That was the first and last time I had a one night stand."

"I never heard from him until three months later when I saw him leaving out of your mother's apartment. Later on I found out he was a close friend of Reginald, who had been your mother's boyfriend for two years at that point. At first I didn't think anything of it, but when he came around I could see she acted different. When she got pregnant no one ever questioned who your father was because we all assumed it was Reginald, but when I saw your eyes I knew she was lying. Those eyes are very rare and only a few people living have them. Your father is one of them."

Mox rubbed his head. He was trying to absorb all this new information he was being told. It made perfect sense when he thought about it. His eyes were distinctive and Reginald sure didn't have eyes like his. He thought back on him and Reginald's relationship and how they never really bonded like a true father and son. They had no similar qualities and nothing in common.

“So what happened the night my mother got murdered?” he asked.

Sybil went on. “Reginald and that man in the picture did a robbery at the world trade center a week before your mother was killed. They stole two million dollars in cash and one million in jewels. Reginald convinced your father to stash everything in Wanda’s apartment. The night before the murder your mother and I got into a huge fight about some money and a lot of foul things were said. That was when she came clean about going behind my back and lying about who your real father was. She told me she was sorry and she said that she would make it up to me by giving me some of the money that was in her apartment. I didn’t believe her until she showed me what was really there and I tell you, I had never seen so much money in my life.” Sybil’s eyes filled up with tears. “Wanda left out to run to the store and I went back into the apartment and stole the money.”

“What?” Cleo wanted her to repeat herself. “You stole what?”

Sybil ignored her son and finished her story. “The next day they came to get the money and it was gone. I heard him torturing Reginald that night, asking him where the money was. I stood by the door and listened to my sister's cries for help while she was being crucified and it was my fault because I could have helped her, but I didn't." A waterfall of tears flooded her face as she confessed her deepest sins.

Mox kept on staring at the picture. He knew this man. "Are you sure *this* is my father?" he questioned.

"Yes I'm sure, Mox. Why?"

The room was silent.

"Because... I know this man."

Earl was surprised. "What?"

Mox studied the photo. "His name is Priest and I shared a cell with him when I was upstate."

"Oh, my God!" Sybil broke down and tried to cover her face from humiliation.

"So, what you tellin' me is... my father is the one who killed my mother that night?"

Sybil's wails became gut wrenching screams for forgiveness and Earl tried to embrace his nephew to console him.

Mox pushed him back. “Don’t fuckin’ touch me. Y’all knew this shit all this time.” He crumbled the picture up in his hand. “I asked you over and over again; both of y’all lied to me. Both of y’all knew the truth from the beginning and you had me runnin’ around killin’ myself tryna figure this shit out. You don’t know half the shit I went through searching for something that was right up under my nose.” He squeezed the crumbled photo harder in his fist.

Suddenly, *‘Breaking News’* flashed across the screen and caught their attention.

Casey Daniels was a prominent prospect out of Westchester County that was headed to the NBA before his life was so suddenly cut short. At twenty one years of age, Casey was shot dead and robbed of his money and jewelry, here at the Marriott hotel at New Roc City last year.

In the winter of that same year, the body of Tamika Hutchins was found on the side of the road by the Roanoke River in Virginia. Police say Hutchins and an accomplice lured Daniels into a room at the hotel and robbed him at gunpoint and then shot him six times, ending his life.

Police have found a missing security tape from the night of Casey Daniels murder at the hotel and they have identified Hutchins' accomplice as this man,

They showed a mug shot of the shooter on Sybil's 37 inch flatscreen.

Twenty six year old; Cleo Daniels. Authorities are advising anyone with information on Mr. Daniels' whereabouts to please contact our crime hotline immediately at 914 -555-5555. Beware, Mr. Daniels is considered armed and very dangerous.

By the time they all turned their heads to look at Cleo his pearl handled, chrome .9 millimeter Ruger was pointed in their direction. He saw Mox reaching for his waist. "You try to pull that shit out and I'ma empty this clip."

"Cleo, why?" Sybil cried.

"Nephew, calm down..."

"Fuck that nephew shit. I know the truth!"

"What truth? What the fuck are you talkin' about?" Earl tried to get Cleo to settle down.

Through sobs, Sybil uttered, "He's adopted."

Mox and Earl replied in unison. *"Adopted?"*

Cleo waved the gun at Mox. "Yeah, adopted." he pointed his finger at Sybil. "That's not my mother, he ain't my uncle and you damn sure ain't my cousin." he clenched his teeth and gave Mox the coldest ice grill he could muster. "I never did like you nigga."

"Why you do it, Cleo?" Mox had known there was another person present at the shooting, but he would have never imagined it to be someone he thought was family.

Sybil and Earl could do nothing but watch as Cleo put the barrel of the gun to Mox's head. "Because, I never liked that lil' nigga, he stole my dream. I was supposed to be the one going to the league, not him."

"That's what this shit is all about. You killed my little brother. He loved you Cleo. We all love you."

"Fuck your love Mox! From day one you always thought you was better than me. Every girl I liked wanted to be with you..." a tear fell from Cleo's eye. "You knew I liked Priscilla and you still went after her!"

Mox was dumfounded. "Priscilla? Nigga, since we was babies I been holding your punk ass down. Everything you was scared to do, I did... and I always gave you the credit. I showed you genuine love, Cleo. Fuck if we aint blood family, we grew up together. We struggled together. We ate and fought together, but all this time you had larceny in your heart towards me. People always told me that, too. They used to say, *'watch your back because your cousin is a snake'*, but I never believed it. I see for myself now. It's always the ones closest to you that hurt you the most."

"Don't bitch up now nigga. I wouldn't have to do this if those fuckin' Italians would've done what they were supposed to do." Cleo cocked the weapon back. "Yeah... I *was* the one who paid drunk Sunny to shoot up the bar and say your name. I figured they could take care of you and I could take care of them, but things didn't go as planned so I gotta do this shit myself, just like I did Casey."

Mox jumped up and tried to grab the gun out of Cleo's hand and a tussle ensued. They wrestled until they hit the ground, but Cleo still had firm grip on the pistol. Mox tried to bend his wrist so that he would drop it, but nothing was working. Cleo was using his 100 pound weight difference to his advantage.

"Cleo stop!" Sybil begged. Earl tried to help, but Cleo backed him up by aiming the gun at him.

The butt end of the Ruger came down on Mox's jaw and the struggle turned one sided.

Cleo made it to his feet and stood over Mox as he lay on the floor, wounded. "Since you miss your brother so bad, I'm 'bout to send you to meet him." he closed his eyes and squeezed the trigger.

The livery cab could barely make it into the parking lot because of all the police cars that were lined up. Priscilla looked out the window as she waited for her change. Paramedics and EMT's were rushing someone to the ambulance on a gurney. She hadn't paid it too much mind until she saw Mox's aunt Sybil and his uncle Wise Earl running alongside the men pushing the small bed on wheels.

She quickly pushed the cab door open and sprang from the seat. All she could see were tubes coming out the mouth of whoever was lying on the gurney. As she got closer, her heart beat faster and faster. She looked at the horror on Sybil's face and knew something was wrong.

When the paramedics whizzed by her it was as if a video frame was playing in slow motion. She saw the only man she ever loved, stretched across a thin mattress, fighting for his life. She reached out to grab his hand, but could only brush his finger-tips because they were moving fast.

Priscilla looked up and then she looked around for her daughter. She didn't see her anywhere. The white and red truck with the flashing lights started to pull away and Priscilla jumped back in the cab.

"Hurry up, follow the ambulance!"

~THE UNION~

26838007R00164

Made in the USA
Charleston, SC
20 February 2014